To: Steve

NDLOVU!

The White Elephant

Hope You Enjoy the read.

P.A

Peter Good

PNEUMA SPRINGS PUBLISHING UK

First Published in 2011 by:
Pneuma Springs Publishing

Ndlovu - The White Elephant
Copyright © 2011   Peter Good

Peter Good has asserted his/her right under the Copyright, Designs
and Patents Act, 1988, to be identified as Author of this Work

Pneuma Springs

British Library Cataloguing in Publication Data

Good, Peter.
  Ndlovu : the white elephant.
  1. Police--Zimbabwe--Fiction. 2. Ex-police officers--
  Zimbabwe--Fiction. 3. Zimbabwe--Social conditions--1980-
  --Fiction. 4. Murder--Investigation--Zimbabwe--Fiction.
  I. Title
  823.9'2-dc22

  ISBN-13: 9781907728228

Pneuma Springs Publishing
A Subsidiary of Pneuma Springs Ltd.
7 Groveherst Road, Dartford Kent, DA1 5JD.
E: admin@pneumasprings.co.uk
W: www.pneumasprings.co.uk

NDLOVU!

The White Elephant

DEDICATION

To my Darling wife Cheryl – without whose insistence, this would never have been written.

To ALL those members of the then British South Africa Police Force, especially the late Gus Armstrong.

FOREWORD

The first rays of light from the rising of the sun over the distant hills shone their feint golden rays onto the whitewashed house nestled between the green trees on the opposing hillside, through the open window, through the gauze fly screen and lit up the figures on the bed in the bedroom. Away in the distance a cockerel crowed, immediately its crow was answered by others, some closer, some even more distant, that their crows could barely be heard.

Tony and Cheryl lay side by side. As the sun's rays settled on their faces, little drops of sweat could clearly be seen on Tony's face, his face twitched and his eyes moved behind their eyelids. Slowly, gradually his body started to twitch, and then suddenly in one movement, his body jumped- eyes opened wide and he let out a yell - "NO, no - you bastards- I will get you..., if it's the last thing I do... You murderous swine...yeah you too Ngonga...you can't hide from me... I will get you...so help me...." as the vivid nightmare, that had now haunted him for years woke him once more, and Cheryl–woken by it all cradled his body next to hers as she tried once again to hush his vivid dream in soothing words, as she gently hugged him close to her. She had had to do this so often now since their marriage that she was becoming adept at it–though she wished with all her heart that these dreams would leave him. For her too–watching him going through this reminded her of how she had had to cope with her own troubled thoughts every time that Tony had had to go out on an anti-terrorist operation when he was still in the Police Force, prior to their marriage.

This was the British South African Police Force, which was the Police Force, of Rhodesia (now Zimbabwe), which is situated between Zambia and Malawi to the North, South Africa and Botswana to the South and West, and Mozambique to the East.

Tony slowly calmed down, "Thanks Honey" he said to her "sorry I woke you again" he apologized, "That's O.K." Cheryl replied "I just wish you would get over those damn memories sweetheart–they drain you so...go and sit down and I will make you a coffee" she added as he got up from the bed and walked out to the lounge. He sat down on his favorite armchair, looking out over the mine where he was now the Compound Manager. He watched as the sun's rays crept over the hills and its light touched the housing of the African miners' village. As he sat there and watched this, he gazed inwards, and saw on the wall his police plague which he had been given on his retirement from the British South Africa Police, together with a crystal beer tankard and an engraved coffee mug, some six months ago. He wiped beads of sweat from his face from the recurrent nightmare he had had ever since his leaving. He could still clearly see the brutally butchered bodies of those loyal African policemen who had served under his control, at the Mambali police post situated on the banks of the Shashe River.

He shuddered, and brought his gaze once again out of the window, where the magnificent sun's rays were now lighting up the whole scene before him, and slowly the nightmare diminished from his memory. Cheryl came over, and placed a cup of coffee on the table by his side, and she stood behind him, and once again, slowly massaged his neck and shoulders, as she always did on these occasions, when he had these vivid nightmares. She felt the tenseness subside and went back to the bedroom. He sat there for a while, slowly drinking his coffee and as he did so, his memory drifted back - back to the very start - it was as clear as yesterday. The start of his fabulous career in the British South African Police Force that he had so loved–and had so waited to take up, once he had passed out from his initial training in the Salisbury Depot.

His mind took over, as he sat looking out over the landscape, and he could recall it all...once again, so clearly as if it had just happened...

And his mind went back, all the way back to his leaving the training Depot, after receiving his posting...

PART ONE

1

There was tapping on the door and Tony woke immediately. The steady swaying of the train's carriage and the "Clickety click" of the wheels on the track brought Tony to his senses.

He had left Salisbury, the Capital City of Rhodesia, the previous evening, on his posting to Matabeleland Province.

He was now on his way to Bulawayo - Rhodesia's second biggest City. He still could not believe that his six month police intensive training course was finally over. As much as he had enjoyed or perhaps endured the training, he could not wait to get into what he had been waiting for–the actual police work and what made him happiest of all was the fact that he had been assigned as a "District policeman" as opposed to being a "Town policeman". This would mean his going to one of the smaller towns or isolated areas, he relished this because he was born in Kenya and had been brought up in various out of the way places. His childhood memories of living in a "mud and wattle" building, lying at night listening to the mournful baying of the hyenas, followed by their almost giggle like sounds, or the roar of a lion in the distance, and the calls of jackals - even the chirping of crickets were noises that he had grown up with and loved to listen to–the sounds of Africa.

He remembered standing on a galvanized iron bath with his older brother David and watching as a herd of elephants went down to the Mara river to drink their fill, mingling with the zebra, wildebeests, gazelles and Rhinos–these were the peaceful serene scenes of Africa that he would always cherish. How dearly he loved the Africa that he had been born into–its ways, its peoples its vastness and animals–these were things that would remain forever with him, within him–for he was truly 'African' regardless of being of European origin–Africa was and would always be–his homeland.

The tapping continued shattering his memories and brought him back to reality. "Yes" he replied from within his two bunk apartment. The voice from the other side said "Coffee or Tea?" After choosing coffee the door was opened and an immaculately dressed Rhodesian Railways Steward entered with a piping hot cup of coffee. "We will be in Bulawayo in approximately two hours" he stated as he placed the cup of coffee down and continued, "the dining car is open for breakfast" and with that he closed the door and proceeded down the next compartments, where the tapping continued, and so on till he was out of earshot.

Tony rose, moved to the foot of the bunk, opened the wash basin and washed his face with cold water....that woke him up and got the sleep from his eyes!

He sat down again had his cup of coffee and then dressed in his starched khaki summer uniform, as he did so he got the whiff of perfume and his memories of the journey that night from Salisbury flooded back.

Having said good-bye to his parents, brothers and sister at the station, as the train got under way he had gone down from his apartment, down to the dining car, and onto the bar.

It was whilst sitting there having a cold glass of Lion Lager that he had got into conversation with a stunning brunette called Felicity. He remembered how they had got on well during the trip as they took their drinks to a vacant table, and were able to look out of the train window, and see townships, and villages pass by, and as the train stopped at each "station" how the multitude of African children would swarm round cheerily waving and holding out their hands, those accustomed to this always brought along plenty of sweets which they tossed out of the window, and the children happily scrambled to pick up as many as they could, shouting their "thanks" as they did so.

Tony recalled how he had walked Felicity back to her apartment later that evening, and the embrace and kiss that had followed... and how they eventually made their way to his compartment, they sat for a while till Tony had slowly put his arms around her, she did not draw back, and they kissed passionately, he slowly lifted her onto the bunk, and slowly caressed her, but as his passion got inflamed- she had suddenly said 'No...please no–not now...' as Tony enquired why, she replied ' Tony, we have only met...you don't even know me and the circumstances of my being on this train' and Tony his passion dampened–gave into her, and said ' Sure, sorry–I just got out of control...' before he could continue she reached over and got off the bunk, she straightened herself and realigned her clothing, kissed him tenderly and thanked him for the drinks and company they had shared and then quietly slipped out of his apartment, and made her way back down to her own apartment ..." aah, that no doubt accounted for the perfumed smell still clinging to my uniform" Tony mused to himself.

He put on his boots and leggings, and his belt and brace, all of which had been highly "spit and polished" to a glasslike finish by his batman-Elliott, for his pass out parade. "Heck" Tony said out aloud "glad that was over" and he could recall the marching, arms drill, Morning P.E... "Yuk" he recalled how that had been what he liked least of all, and of course all the lectures on Law and Order. He was so happy to have finally made it!

Once fully dressed Tony proceeded down the corridor from his apartment, down the swaying carriages to the dining car which he noticed was already filling up.

He noticed Felicity right away, and she was sitting with two young children–he remembered that last night she had mentioned them, which is why she could not invite him into her apartment. "Look Mummy" the one said "a policeman". Felicity beckoned Tony over to them and on his arrival invited him to join them at their table, he accepting her offer sat down.

The Steward came over and took his order; he opted for the full breakfast- fried eggs, bacon, tomato mushrooms, toast, marmalade and a pot of coffee.

Having placed his order Tony turned to the children and said "Hi-Kids-going to Bulawayo then are you?" he asked.

Their faces lit up – the policeman was actually talking to THEM. They set about telling Tony that, not only were they going to Bulawayo, but from there they were taking the train bound for Johannesburg in South Africa, and from there going onto Durban where they were joining their grandparents for a holiday "because our Daddy was killed" they added matter-of-factly. Tony's heart went out to them and to Felicity, as he remembered that during their long conversation the previous night over drinks how she had told him how her husband had died in a plane - "dusting" a farmer's field. And now he could understand her hesitance in his apartment last night, and not only could he clearly now accept it, but deep down inside he felt quite a cad for even attempting his 'move' on her!

When she and the children had finished their breakfast, she rose and slipping a piece of paper into Tony's hand said "That's our address - if you want to drop us a line" and with that she left and returned to her apartment.

Tony finished his breakfast and slowly walked back down the swaying carriages towards his apartment, taking in the scenic sight of the vast open veldt as he did so. Others too were doing just that, leaning out of the windows in the carriages, and having to step back into their apartments to allow Tony to get by.

Getting back to his apartment, he meticulously packed has case and kit bag, ensuring that nothing had been left out. Having done that he stepped out into the passageway and leant out of the window, the wind blowing in his face as he looked out at the land, the grass already dried to a yellowish brown, watching the hills and trees roll by as he wondered just where he might be posted to, and just what lay ahead for him.

2

Arriving at the Bulawayo Railway station, Tony found that an African Constable driver, and a Landrover were waiting for him, and he was then taken to the main police station which also included the Headquarters for the Matabeleland Province.

He noticed Bulawayo, had really wide streets, it was said that they were so designed in the days prior to motor vehicles, and were made that wide to enable a span of oxen and a cart to turn in the streets with ease. Of course now with the progress of time, the center part of the streets were used for parking spaces, as were the sides of the streets, and these were regularly patrolled by the towns traffic wardens.

They stood out, dressed in their deep royal blue uniforms.

The Landrover sped on, and eventually turned into the main police station, and came to a halt. Tony stepped out, and walked over to the Central Charge Office, and was directed to the Officer Commanding, Bulawayo District's Office, a Chief Superintendent Sam Wheller.

He knocked, entered came smartly to a halt and saluted.

Mr. Wheller looked up from his desk, and when Tony gave his name and serial Number, Mr. Wheller looked up again, "Umm... Ah yes, you're posted to the District Gwanda, you will be going in a week, till then, have the driver take you to the police camp and report to the 'Riot Squad'...might as well make use of you, till your posting...dismissed' Tony saluted, and walked out, back to the Landrover, and had the driver take him to the Bulawayo police camp.

Tony spent a week in the "Riot Squad" patrolling the Bulawayo townships, before getting his first posting to district police life.

His first post had been to the town of Gwanda - South of Bulawayo on the main road to Beitbridge – the border crossing point from Rhodesia to South Africa. Not having his own transport at this stage Tony had been given a ticket to catch the Rhodesian Railways Coach to Gwanda and the start of his life as a 'district policeman'.

He was greeted, as he got off the coach, by Constable Johnny Johnson, who was waiting for him, and with whom he developed a great friendship over the years to come. Constable Johnson took him back to the Gwanda mess, where he was introduced to the other Constables, and then showed to his room. The 'mess' resembled a large house, big verandah at the front, the lounge to the left, behind the lounge was the dining room, and behind that the kitchen. Off the verandah were two bedrooms, then on the right hand side of the verandah was Tony's bedroom, behind his was a further bedroom, behind that there were the toilets, and then finally the bathroom and showers. Tony unpacked, neatly placing his uniform into the cupboard, together with his own personal clothes, and he changed into a pair of jeans, and checked shirt, and slipping on some 'tennis shoes' went back to the lounge to join the others.

In the next few years he was to fall in love with the district way of life. This is what he was born into, and what he loved. His patrols being of two week duration, whether on cycle, horseback or Landrover took him into the African "homelands", and with his camping out in tents sitting around a camp fire, he soon had his African policemen teach him the local dialect, which in this part of the country was Sindebele - Tony was a quick learner and under their expert guidance, could soon speak the language fluently. This was to stand him in good stead in the years to come.

After just a year at Gwanda, Tony was transferred some two hundred miles, north of Bulawayo, to the Wankie police station.

Whilst stationed at the Wankie police station, which was a coal mining area, the main colliery, was within the town area itself, with great hills of coal dust giving off a pungent smell. The area had housing for the miners, a club and swimming pool facilities plus local stores. Whilst at Wankie he had frequent opportunities to visit the famed Victoria Falls, and on each time he could find something new to catch his attention and could but wonder how David Livingstone must have looked on in awe at this untamed spectacle, the sound of which could be clearly heard, miles before you came upon it. He could understand why it was such a tourist attraction. Whilst at Wankie he would also patrol, down to the Zambezi River area, little knowing at that time, how years later this area around Mana Pools would become one of the worst 'hot-beds' of terrorist fighting. He also had patrols that took him into the Wankie Game Reserve, and these he loved, for once again, like in his childhood days, he was surrounded by herds of impalas, wildebeests, zebra, buffaloes, elephants, prides of lions, together with cheaters, rhinos and even leopards and hyenas. Little did he know that he himself would be named one of these animal names by a local African chief–not mockingly, but out of deep respect, after an Elephant!

Unfortunately Tony left this station under a "cloud". He had got engaged to a girl, whose father was known to be "fond of the drink", and it was when the Officer Commanding had confronted Tony with this, that Tony had exploded "So what? I am not going to be marrying the father, you ****!!!" and having swore, left without even being dismissed and without the customary salute due to an Officer.

He found himself that same night, being put on a train back to Bulawayo, where once again on his arrival he found himself back on "Riot Squad" duty for the next two weeks whilst awaiting his next posting, and his biggest fear was that he might end up, back in town as a town policeman - something he definitely did not like!

He duly reported to the main police station, to be given his next posting, which was, thankfully, to be the police station of Kezi - way out in the "bush". So far out–that the police station did not even have electricity, so he might as well try and sell anything electrical now before going, but rather than being disappointed, Tony was elated at the prospect. 'Heck' he said to himself 'this will be like being back in Kenya again–better get myself a battery operated radiogram, so I can play my records' he mused.

After getting his "orders" he was walking down the corridor, when he just happened to look into one of the offices and saw a face that he recognized.

He stopped, turned and looked again, and on seeing that he was right, without thinking or knocking walked straight into the office, at the desk sat his former Inspector whom he had served under as a police Cadet whilst stationed at Highfields police station in Salisbury–Gus Armstrong.

"Hiya Mr. Armstrong" Tony said, and Gus, immediately recognizing Tony stood up extending his right arm, and warmly shook hands with Tony (Who - had not even noticed that Gus was now an Officer–a Superintendent and was in fact due a salute!)

"Well, well Woody" Gus said "What is all this I hear about you up in Wankie, eh?" And after listening to Tony's account of the matter, which no one else had been willing to do, said "Well - I hear that you are being posted to Kezi - well you might as well know that I am going to be the new Officer Commanding the Gwanda Area, and Kezi will be under my control. So, Woody, come on, pull your socks up lad, and let's have you back on even keel again shall we...come on Woody, I know that you have what it takes to make a good policeman." Tony felt at last, that his police career was changing for the better, and that with Gus as his Officer Commanding, he would at last have an Officer that would be both fair, and deserving of respect.

Tony, had by this time, bought his older brother David's Ford Zodiac, and he followed the road to Kezi, taking him through the Matopos area, where upon one of the hills, called 'view of the world', lay the burial place of Cecil John Rhodes, the founder of Rhodesia. The tarmac strip eventually gave out to a dirt road that finally led him to the small village of Kezi. He drove up to the police station, and went and presented himself to Inspector Larry King, and then proceeded to the police mess to settle himself in. Under the guidance of the Inspector at Kezi, who had called Tony to one side and had told him "Just remember lad, no matter how much scrambled egg they may have on their cap, if you take away their uniform- they are just like you and I. BUT, remember, once they are in uniform, no matter how stupid they may act, or silly a thing they may say- don't go off at them- without first saying WITH DUE RESPECT, SIR - and then let them have it..., there is nothing they can do, IF you have given them the due respect bit."

This was something that Tony would always bear in mind, and under the guidance of this Inspector, Tony soon rose to Second In Charge of the station, and as a Public Prosecutor at the local court, a job that he really relished and soon got the reputation of being a "Perry Mason" winning almost all his cases, even the defended ones at that!

There were many amusing times, like the one time, when a case of Stock Theft came before him to prosecute, that when the judge was seated, the defense attorney rose and said that the accused had not been given the opportunity to identify the beast in question - so the court had to be adjourned, all had to travel some fifty miles to the stock pens where the beast was being held, Tony travelling with the Defense Attorney, in the Defense Attorneys car.

When they got there, the Complainant, was first brought in and asked to identify his beast, within a few minutes of overlooking all the beasts in the stock pen, he walked up and rightly identified the beast. The accused was then brought in, and asked to identify "his beast". He took many minutes of carefully walking about in the pen, looking at all the beasts, before turning to his defense attorney and saying "They have not brought it out!"

His case was SHOT!! But to add insult to injury- on the return trip the exhaust fell of the attorney's car, and five miles from the main road, the fan went through the radiator! Tony and the Attorney had to wait till a tow truck could come and tow them back, by this time, the Magistrate, who was known to look forward to his "sundowner" drink each evening, was pacing up and down- as it was well past six in the evening. With lights on in the court room, run from a generator, after Tony had done a quick "sum up" the Attorney rose to try and put forward a defense, only to have the Magistrate but in and say "really, is there any point in this–in light of what happened at the stock pen?" to which the Attorney had to say NO, and as he sat down the accused was found guilty and sentenced to five years, and Tony cheeky as ever turned to the Attorney, patting him on the shoulder and said "Good case to win, eh?" and walked out– leaving the Attorney to make inquiries as to how to get himself back to Bulawayo some fifty miles away!!!

There was the time that Tony was woken at 2am in the morning, to go to the office, for an African policeman to ask if Tony could take a man he had arrested for the possession of "dagga" (Cannabis) to the Hospital for an x-ray. When Tony had asked "Why?" the Constable replied "He swallowed the evidence–an x-ray will show it up in his stomach" …notwithstanding the nearest Hospital with such facilities was fifty miles away in Bulawayo! This same Constable had once filled out in his patrol report that while cycling down one road he had come across a pride of lions, and he stated that he had slowly got off his cycle, pulled his helmet down over his face so that the lions would not be able to see him!!!

After a spell of relieving the Member In Charge of the Fort Rixon police station, Tony was given the job as Member In Charge of the Gwanda District Stock Theft Section, which saw him spend many a fine time at Beitbridge police station. This was the immigration post between South Africa and Rhodesia, and Tony was able to spend many nice evenings at Messina in South Africa, the first town one came to on entering South Africa, it had a nice drive-in Cinema, of which Tony took full advantage.

There was also a lovely mining club house, where film shows were also shown, as well as dances. It was on the occasion of a big dance, that Tony, having befriended a Beitbridge resident who owned an old Rolls Royce, who as a joke had Tony dress in his best suit, and the owner dressed as a chauffeur, and with Tony sitting in the back, with the interior lights on, drove him to the dance. On arrival at the club house, they had all those there wondering just who the "dignitary" was!!!

He also had a week at Tuli police station, where his friend nick-named "Kudu Ears" (after a large antelope - which had large protruding ears) was in charge. Kudu was quite mad, and many a jaunt was made up close to herds of elephant which at times completely surrounding them.

He also came upon some odd cases and one such one was a report of a death. Tony and one of his African Constables proceeded to the "kraal" (the African home) where the death had occurred, and there found the deceased lying quite naked, just within the kraal grounds. On speaking to the dead man's wife it transpired that he and his wife were sitting down to their evening meal when they heard the cries of a young girl. The husband got up and went out and found, up the path a very distressed young girl. When he asked her what the problem was she had replied that she had been on her way home, when she was accosted by some TOGALOSH (the African equivalent of the Irish leprechauns- "little people"). Now although the wife was a believer in these, the husband was not, and so he offered to walk the young girl home, which he did, explaining to the girl's father what had happened - the girl's father also believing in these "little people" was in horror - saying that the husband should not have intervened, as the Togalosh would now leave his daughter and come after her helper instead. The Husband scoffed at this, and returned to his kraal where he recounted all to his wife, who herself now had bad feelings of what would now befall her husband, fearing for his safety.

They went to bed and at 2am the next morning she awoke to find her husband dressing. On asking what he was doing, he had replied that he was going to see a friend that lived on the other side of the dam that separated their kraals. She had told him not to go but rather to wait till daylight, but he had laughed at her and left - as she stated having been called by the Togalosh!

Anyway at daylight, she went out to get some milk from the cows, and found her husband lying where he was- completely naked and as dead as a dodo!

Tony had the body taken back to Gwanda for a post-mortem- which was carried out but could reveal no cause of death, so certain parts of the body were taken and sent to the Path-Lab in Salisbury for examination to ascertain the cause of death.

Tony eagerly awaited the reply....which duly came in about a week's time, with, under the cause for death, there was written:" NO KNOWN CAUSE OF DEATH COULD BE FOUND."

So...as his Constable quickly pointed out ...it must have been the...TOGALOSH!!!

It was whilst investigating the theft of cattle from the Champion and Nazeby ranches belonging to Bison Pritzkow that Tony got a real good result, ending in the arrest and subsequent conviction of fourteen local Africans — and resulted in Tony and Bison becoming firm friends. Consequently on his promotion Tony was offered the position of Member In Charge of the new police station built on the site of the old SUN YET SEN Mine - the police station adopting the name SUN YET SEN - which was only some five miles from the Nazeby Ranch.

It was whilst at this station that Tony was to be given his well earned nickname, by the local African Chief and got to be known by the African populace.

The name was given to him, NOT because of his portly figure, but because of his relentless pursuit of criminal, and never ever giving up till he got a conclusion.

So they gave him the name to which he would be called by those endeared to him, and by those too, who would be in fear of him...which when translated into English meant...Elephant.

Yes it was here that Tony became...NDLOVU - the White Elephant!!! (Ndlovu was an accepted word from the Ndebele word Mandlovu used by people other than Ndebele, conveying the same meaning — Elephant.)

3

Ngonga cycled up to the kraal in Matopos where Maduma was holding the "beer drink"- the gathering was already in full swing. Ngonga got off his new Raleigh cycle - the cycle along with a plaque with the police Badge on it with an inscription that read "Constable Ngonga - for excellent service. We will miss your knowledge." It was signed "Section Officer Tony (Ndlovu) Wood, and all the members of the Sun Yet Sen police station - wishing you a happy retirement."

He was proud of this; his service under "Ndlovu" had been a very happy one. Although he had sat for promotion to Sergeant, twice and failed, Ngonga knew that under Section Officer Wood, his police investigative skills were recognized, but more importantly, valued too, and that made up for his not getting promoted. The new cycle was a present too from all those at Sun Yet Sen - so he had many happy memories to cherish during his retirement.

He was a tall, strong man, kept fit from his twenty years service in the Police Force. He had a fine built body, still not so much as an inch of fat. He was still single, though he knew that in the Sun Yet Sen area, where he had spent his last years of service, he had for sure fathered many children, with many different women! That was, he thought, his privilege of being single and in demand!

He walked up into the gathering, Maduma had known Ngonga for years, and the "beer drink" was in a way in honor to this ex policeman, to welcome him back to their area where they hoped to spend pleasant times together.

As Ngonga approached the circle of men sitting down, attended to by the womenfolk, he immediately made eye contact with a young plumpish woman, who smiled back at him, at once making his heart to race as he instinctively thought how having sex with her would be a pleasure although, of course, the thought of marriage would be furthermost from his mind!

As she brought the calabash of beer round the circle of men, on reaching to hand it to Ngonga, he made sure that his hands overlapped hers, and he held them pressed onto the calabash for several seconds whilst he looked into her eyes smiling as he said "Thank you ", before accepting the beer and finally letting her go. As he watched her go, he already had stirrings in his groin for this woman.

As the evening wore on, and the beer flowed, Ngonga approached this woman, and without beating about the bush, which was his manner in these circumstances, as he spoke to her he bluntly said "How about coming back to my house, when this is over, and spending the night with me?" His tone and sneer made it quite obvious what he had in mind, and caused the young woman to giggle, and then she replied "Oh...no....no...I could not." She looked down at her feet which she shuffled about, shyly.

Ngonga tried to reason with her, telling her what a 'not to be missed offer' he was making, after all he was Ngonga, the stud, and once again he repeated his "offer" to her, which she again shyly refused, and with his ego blunted, he turned sharply saying "Bitch" and walked off briskly, and returned to the circle of men at the beer drink, one thing about Ngonga - he did not take rejection kindly.

It was past midnight that Ngonga, still ever watchful, saw the young woman leave the kraal area, and walk out into the darkness beyond the burning fires. He knew that she was going into the thicket, to "relieve" herself, and already in his mind's eye he could picture the sight, and immediately again those old familiar stirrings in his groin started again!

Downing his last sup of beer, he stood up, saying to those in the circle that he had to go and relieve himself, and slowly started walking away from the gathering, but so as not to get any in the circle thinking the obvious, he walked in the opposite direction to that taken by the young girl.

Once he had got out of the light of the fires, where he could not be clearly observed, Ngonga slowly circled the kraal and walked over to the thicket of bushes, where he knew the woman would have gone to.

He crept up into this area, and there in the moonlight he saw her. She squatted, with her dress hoisted up to her waist, and as often the case, not having any underwear on, she was naked from the waist down, she sat relieving herself, as Ngonga watched in awe the desire of having sex with her increasing within him.

She suddenly turned, and gasped as she suddenly realized that Ngonga was there watching her, and stood up, her dress falling back down.

Ngonga laughed and said "Don't stop because of me...I too am having a pee" and with that he undid his flies and released his already erect, large manhood in her sight, and started to try and pass water.

There was little he could do, as he was not ready to do that, but rather he was so aroused and really only had one thing on his mind, so as the woman was preparing to walk off, he grabbed her arm, turning her toward him, his erect manhood standing out like his old police baton! Again he repeated his interest in her, proposing that they lie down right there in the thicket, where no one could see them, and enjoy sex together.

She again struggled against his grasp, and said "NO".

But by now, not only angered by her continual rejection, which he could not understand - no one had EVER rejected his advances before, just the opposite, they had all been only to pleased to accommodate him - but also spurred on by his sexual arousal, that he made a grab for her dress, which he viciously tugged at, and tore off from her waist, leaving her once again naked from the waist down.

She started a scream, but his hand clasped her mouth so that nothing came out, as he pushed himself and his erect member onto her, manipulating his member so that it started to penetrate her.

She struggled violently and for a minute broke free from him, and again tried to call out, but once again, Ngonga jumped over to her side, and this time colliding with her knocked her to the ground. She let out a cry of surprise, which did not carry far, and in an instant Ngonga was upon her, hand over her mouth muffling any further cries as he sneeringly said "Don't be stupid, young woman, I know that you will enjoy me- all the woman do, now just lie there and let me fill you with the joy of my lovemaking." Such was his ego on the sexual level.

As he once more penetrated her, she now in panic, opened her mouth, his little finger fell into the open mouth and she realized here was a chance, she had to take, so she bit down hard as she could on his finger, feeling her teeth tear through the skin.

Ngonga gave a yelp of his own, and the sudden anger of his being so stubbornly being utterly rejected by this woman, coupled with the vast amount of beer he had consumed, overtook his judgment all together. Without thinking, he reached down, to the large hunting knife that he always carried with him, pulling it from its sheath; he began to strike at the woman with it.

21

The knife cut deep into the young woman's throat, severing the artery and the blood gashed out. He still had his other hand over her mouth and he suddenly felt the warmth of her blood spurting onto his arm and running down to his hand. He moved, and as he did so, she let out a blood curdling scream, which had Ngonga bring the knife back, up and down upon her body in a series of wicked blows, which not only ended her life, but which horribly mutilated her young body.

It took a few minutes for Ngonga to suddenly realize just what he had done. The sheer brutality of what he had just done, the anger that he had vented out on this poor young woman, made him stop and gather his thoughts. "My God "he thought to himself "I have just committed a MURDER - not to mention the attempted rape". He dressed himself and realizing that her last screams must have been heard by those over at the kraal, at the beer drink, for he already heard excited voices calling to one another, and noticed that some bearing torches, and hurricane lamps, were already heading over in his direction.

He replaced the hunting knife; the blade still covered in blood, back into its sheath, and quickly ran off into the darkness.

He left his new cycle, the present he had received, at Maduma's kraal, and ran as quick as he could, through the night, back to his own home.

Once he had got home, he washed, changed his clothes, and gathered up all the money that he had, and already, his head clearing- he was formulating what he must do.

He left his home, and walked briskly down the road, down to the local shopping area and bus station.

He knew that the first bus would arrive at 5am. He knew too that Maduma and those with him, would by now have discovered the murdered body of the young woman, and although it would take some time to realize that he was missing, by the time that they put two and two together, and get to the nearest police station at Matopos to report the crime, he would be well on his way away from here on the bus.

At 5am on schedule, the bus pulled up, and Ngonga got one ticket for the Antelope mine, which was halfway between Kezi and Sun Yet Sen. The bus dropped him off at the Antelope Mine Store, and Ngonga relaxed, for here he was in an area that he was familiar with, and with people he knew, most of whom would not yet know that he had in fact left the Police Force, and he would use this to his advantage.

It was on the third day in the Sun Yet Sen area, enjoying the hospitality of the locals that Ngonga first got wind of the news of the "murder" and that Tony (Ndlovu) was on to him.

His heart sank...he knew that Ndlovu had so many reliable sources of information in this area, that his every movement would soon be made known to Ndlovu.

How right he had been. For over the next week, he was constantly "on the run". Sometimes he only just managed to leave an area he was sheltering in, before Ndlovu and Tazwinga (the Sun Yet Sen Sergeant Major) and other policemen arrived.

Ever so slowly he was being pushed down southwards towards Botswana. The police "net" was closing in. Finally, Ngonga realized that he was virtually cut off. He had travelled south, past the Mambali police post, and was now standing on the side of the Shashe river which formed the boundary between Rhodesia and Botswana, and he knew that he had no choice, he either had to cross over - or be caught and be convicted as a criminal, and the thought of being sent to a prison wherein there would be countless criminals that he had in fact been responsible for putting in prison–and what they might do to him– made him shudder. He could not allow that so he slowly strode out into the river, (fortunately–it was not the rainy season, so the river was not in full flow...bank to bank, which no one in their right senses would have attempted to swim in!) and was soon swimming over to the other side, as the river slowly pulled him downstream.

At last his feet struck solid ground, and after a while he was able to emerge on the Botswana side of the river, drenched and exhausted, but now he was smiling, he felt good, he had in fact evaded Ndlovu - no mean feat and he laughed out loudly stating "I beat you, Ndlovu! Here is one you did not get–that will upset your record" and again he gave a loud laugh as he walked into the thicket of bushes by the side of the river, and there he lay down to dry out.

Once dry he got up and headed inwards into Botswana. Little did he realize the chain of events that were to follow that would find him returning to this very spot, but the next time as a senior member of an armed group of terrorists, that would wreak havoc, and as a result, once again, he and his band would be chased, yet again by...NDLOVU...the White Elephant.

4

The sun was setting over the distant hills which now took on a blue colour, casting its last red rays over the barren land dried out by the past two years of drought. The sky was a breathtaking picture - like a wild veldt fire, the different hues of red mingling with the clouds made the sky appear to be on fire, and this reflected onto the windows of the Sun Yet Sen police station's mess.

Sun Yet Sen was set like an oasis in a desert - for here amongst the barren landscape was this police station with its dark green Flame Lilly hedge surrounding the whole camp, with it's magnificent flame Lilly flower - which as the name suggested, was a bright red - matched the setting sunset.

From the mess, which was situated at the top of the hill, the camp was three-tiered down to the Charge Office, which was adjacent to the main, dirt road that ran from the Nazeby Ranch all the way past the Antelope Mine Store, and on up to the Kezi police station at which point the road became a tarmac stripped road, which then ran to Matopos where it became a full tarmac road which ran on into Bulawayo.

Around the mess and on each tier was an invitingly green grassy area, as there was at the front of the Charge Office Building, which extended up to the surrounding flame Lilly hedge.

The road into the police camp, the road off the main road up to the mess, and all round the Charge Office, Prison Cells and the African police Housing, was gravel and marked out by large whitewashed stones, truly making this camp stand out in contrast to its dusty brown surrounds.

Tony stood on the verandah of the mess watching the glowing sunset. He had always been surprised how quickly the sun set, leaving so little time to enjoy its fiery farewell before it sank below the horizon and the darkness, murky grey turning to a deep black, quickly swept in and engulfed the land.

It was then that the night noises that Tony loved so much about Africa and the bush took over. These night noises–be it the chirping of the crickets, those great alarm systems that stopped chirping when someone or something approached them, or the barking of a dog from nearby kraal, or perhaps the baying of a jackal or the mighty roar of a lion in the distance or more so the throaty rasping sound that it gave afterward–these were the night noises that Tony so loved. But there was something else that Tony enjoyed more than anything else and that was the smell of rain!!! Yes, it was the SMELL of the impending rain, a distinctive clean smell–as the first large rain drops hit the parched earth sending up puffs of dust. "Boy, how we could do with some rain right now" Tony mused as his batman Elliott came out onto the verandah with a Tilley lamp. He hung it up, left and re-appeared a few moments later with a frosted glass - which had been chilled in the fridge, and a cold bottle of Lion Lager, which he handed over and was enthusiastically received by Tony. Tony walked over to an armchair and sank down into it, pouring the beer into his glass and began to sip the cold nectar and relax after another day's work.

Tony had been in charge of this station for eight years now and he loved every minute of it.

He recalled how on getting here, the station just having been built, was as barren, dry and dusty as the surrounding area, and how he had put the prisoners to work, layering, grass and hedge planting, and the continual watering that had transformed the station to its present park like state.

Of course he remembered too, how at a Member In Charge's meeting with the Officer Commanding Gwanda Area, held at Gwanda (The Member In Charge of each station, seven in all met each month to discuss any problems and any overall situation that might affect them all) the Officer Commanding Gus Armstrong had brought up the matter of water bills for the past month, stating "Once again almost all stations have exceeded their quota - and Sun Yet Sen, yet again using as much as the other six put together - please S/O Wood, could you please try and ensure that this is remedied forthwith?"

There was only one other Section Officer in Charge of a station, that was "Kudu" from Tuli, the others were Inspectors and Chief Inspectors, who often found Tony's attitude to superior ranks a matter that got under their skins, and so now each of them exchanged knowing glances and wry smiles - but it was "Kudu" who had the biggest smile, when Tony replied "With due respect, sir, as you are aware, the situation at Sun Yet Sen - well it was just a barren waste, as the whole area is, but you are also aware that I have managed to transform it from that barren state to the park like scene that it is now in, this of course has taken, and alas will continue to take a large usage of water, to keep up its appearance...but...no skin off my nose ...I'm quite prepared to let it return to its former state by using less water...but as you know, sir, not only have the local farmers and mission staff, but also the Deputy Commissioner himself commented on its lovely present condition - how it really sticks out from the rest of the area..." he paused, and had to smile as he noticed the look of surprise on the faces of the senior members, at how dare he speak to the Officer Commanding like this–instead of just mildly agreeing...but he had won his way with Gus saying "Yes, Yes, I am aware of that, well...just try and use as little as it takes to keep it in its present state...let's hope for a nice rainy season, that will help."

Of course what none of them realized was the fact that Tony and Gus Armstrong had quickly set up a rapport, which had lasted these past 10 years. In fact there had been many times when Gus had asked Tony to baby-sit his children, not due to any favoritism, but due to the mutual respect that they had for one another, Tony for Gus for the trust and fairness that Gus showed when dealing with him and others, always willing to listen and not just jump to conclusions or to "lord" it over those junior in rank, and "Gus" with Tony, not only for Tony's skill as a policeman, but also for his public prosecutor duties that had been highly commented on by the Senior Magistrate to Gus, but also just for Tony as a trust worthy person.

Tony's thought were interrupted as Rod and Dell appeared and joined him on the verandah. These two Patrol Officers had come to Sun Yet Sen direct from finishing their police training at the Salisbury Depot, and so were just right for Tony to mold into the type of policemen that Tony wanted, and they were already showing, with careful guidance that they could well be good and fair investigators, but more importantly - non racist! This was something that Tony was insistent on. A strange thing to be held by many who were born in Africa, who often felt that they were superior due solely on the colour of their skin! Yet it was a known fact that Tony, learning to speak the African language, had won the respect of the local African Chiefs, their Headmen and more importantly the general African populace together with his African policemen - who under Sergeant Major Tazwinga had seen evidence of Tony's trust and fairness. Tazwinga himself had over the past years built up a special friendship with Tony, and it was readily agreed that the African policemen, would be willing to give their lives for their Member In Charge...if only they knew, how very shortly, some of them would be called upon to do just that !!!

26

5

It was a time of unrest. Ever since the declaration of UDI by the Prime Minister, Mr. Ian Smith, Rhodesia was not only fighting "sanctions" but was now the prime target of terrorists, and Sun Yet Sen with its two sub stations along the border with Botswana (Sear Block and Mambali) were especially vulnerable from terrorist groups that were harboured in Botswana.

These two police posts were easily accessible during the drought and the Shashe River, which formed the boundary between the two countries, was no longer in full flow, therefore anyone could easily cross the river which would only be knee to waist high at most.

The respect that the locals had for Tony was paying off. Anytime bands of terrorists were seen to cross over or contacted the local inhabitants for food or shelter, the news was quickly reported back to Tony by his regular supply of "informers" and the necessary action quickly put into force.

Sometimes this would be purely a police action, calling upon the local police reservists, but on two occasions Tony had to call upon the army units from Bulawayo together with Air-force spotter planes to assist as well.

The one amusing occasion when they had got the terrorists known to be on a hill top, the Army was called in, who took up the position of the "stop line" round the base of the hill, whilst the police had to be the "killing group" to go up the hill from one side. The Army surrounded all other sides, should the terrorists try to flee from the top. Arrangements were made once the Army stopper group was in position, and the police "killer group" was all set to go up the hill, for a spotter plane to fly over at first light to give necessary directions.

All was ready - and as the first rays of light came, sure enough here was the spotter plane, which flew over all those assembled below. The killing group went up - the stop group all on alert to repel any terrorist who came down. As the "killing group" crept further and further up the hill the spotter plane re-appeared, circled once more, then radioed down "You are on the wrong hill!"

The terrorists were on the next hill, most probably watching the events unfurling before their eyes, to the great amusement!

Apart from this occasion, nearly every other incursion of terrorists had met with defeat - with either all the terrorists being killed or captured, but a few managed to flee back to Botswana.

The local African populace, it could be said, were not impressed with these so called "freedom fighters", not only due to the fact that these intimidated the locals, raped their womenfolk young and old, and often forced many of the young men to go unwillingly with them back to training camps, but also due to the fact that those who refused to give them either food or shelter were often killed or mutilated - cases were rife where the ears of loved ones were cut off, cooked and then given to their spouses to eat! There were also occasions too where the cattle of the locals were slaughtered- not for food purposes, but killed or severely maimed just to try and intimidate the owners into following the cause of the "freedom fighters".

Most of the locals of this area were not interested in politics. Their only concern was to get sufficient rains, not only for their livestock, but more so for the sake of getting a good crop. If there was sufficient; their herds healthy, and enough to make their customary "kaffir beer" for their weekly beer drinks, they were happy.

The "kaffir-beer" was brewed in 44 gallon drums. It was a grey-brown colour with a thick scum several inches thick on top, but certainly 100% proof!

When the beer was ready all the men folk would sit in a circle–the owner of the beer-drink would have his wives serve the beer in a calabash, which would be filled, given to the kraal owner who would drink his fill and then pass the calabash on to the person seated on his left, who with a clap of his hands to express his thanks, would accept, drink his fill and pass it on to the one on his left, who would repeat the same procedure and so on till the calabash was empty, when one of the women who would be hovering, would grab it, hand over another full one, taking the empty one back, and dipping it into the 44 gallon drum - after scraping away the scum, and re-fill it, and once again, go over to the circle of men, to be ready to replace the empty one once again, and so the procedure would go on till the 44 gallon drum of beer was finished!

It had at first shocked the local Africans when Tony whilst on his patrols and coming upon a beer drink in progress, had approached the owner, greeted him in the local dialect, and then had gone over and sat down in the "circle" of men folk in the customary way, and then actually joined in the drinking from the calabash, which he had received with the expressed "thanks" by clapping his hands!

It was this act that had endeared him to the local African populace- for here was a "white policeman" who did not look down on them for their difference of colour, and did not just see only bad - but was willing to talk their language, and join in their customs!

It was this aspect that Tony was trying to instill in his two Patrol Officers.

6

The three were sitting in the verandah when their discussion of the day's events was interrupted by the ringing of the telephone. Rod who was the nearest jumped up and answered it, and after a few moments turned towards Tony and said "It's for you - Constable Rhodes at the office." Tony reluctantly put down his glass, sighed and got up.

This was the difference between a District policeman's life as opposed to that of a Town policeman. If you were a Town policeman you would have your regular shift hours, and once you had worked those hours, that was you done for the day. If you had come across a "crime" you would report it and stay on the scene till the squad member who dealt with that particular crime arrived and would take over the investigations into the crime.

A District policeman would start his day at 0600hrs each day with what was called the "stable parade". This dated back to the time when there was a horse at the district stations that was used for horse patrols and at 0600hrs there would be cleaning and feeding of the horse. These days the name stayed- but now the time was used to check over all the transport at the station, making sure that each vehicle was clean, and had oil, water, petrol and checking of battery and tyres and the like. Once that was done, the time was then used to go over any cases that you were working on, or getting cases ready for "Court" making sure you had all the documents to hand, in order ready to be presented, and in general getting the police station ready for the day's events.

Then the District policeman would work on through the day till 1600hrs, when they would finish, BUT, those at the station would then take turns, normally of a week at a time, being "on call" for that week between 1600hrs until 0600hrs the next morning, and the one that was on call, would deal with any crime reports or other incidents that cropped up during those hours.

Tony had arranged this between the three of them, but with Tony being available to assist or give advice to either of the other two if they required it.

Tony crossed over to where Rod stood, and took the receiver from him "Yes–Rhodes - what's the problem?" he inquired. Rhodes replied "Good evening sir, it's Mambali - they have not responded to our last two scheduled calls" he stated.

Mambali was one of the two border posts that came under the command of the Sun Yet Sen station, the two sub posts bordering onto Botswana.

Due to the terrorist threat, Tony had each of these two posts radio in to the main station, on the hour, every hour, so that they would know that all was O.K.

To miss one of these calls could be put down as an oversight, but to miss two - then it was to be assumed that the post had been attacked and the Constables manning it killed.

Although there had been the odd occasion when such was assumed, only for Tony and a squad of specially trained anti terrorist policemen, stationed at Sun Yet Sen, to have gone all the way down to the post- leaving the Landrovers, and walking the last few miles - so as not to alert any "insurgents", only to find on getting there, that everything was in fact OK, just that the Constable "on duty" had in fact fallen asleep.

On such occasions Tony's reactions were mixed - happy to find that the Constables were still alive, but at the same time as mad as a hornet for having come all that way- just to find the offending member asleep!

Still, each occasion such as this, it had to be assumed that the worst had happened, and steps put into motion.

This now was the situation that Tony found himself in, and already his "police" mind was in top gear, formulating plans as he spoke "Thanks, Rhodes please ask Sergeant Major Tazwinga to meet me in my office in ten minutes" and he hung up.

Turning towards Rod and Dell, who were by now eagerly waiting to hear what was up, Tony quickly filled them in as to how the situation stood and said "Rod, will you take the Armoury keys and get sufficient arms and ammo for two Landrover crews?" and without waiting for a reply turned towards Dell and continued "Dell would you take the store keys and get sufficient packs and rations for the crews, for let's say, two weeks each man – OK."

Rod and Dell immediately departed as Tony retired to his bedroom, and pulling out his camouflage gear started to change into them.

Having changed, Tony left the mess and started down towards the office. The now cool night air was refreshing after the hot dry day.

As he walked towards the office block, he looked up at the large silvery moon surrounded by stars, like small glittering diamonds on a backcloth of blue-black, and thought to himself "Trust it to be so clear tonight, we will have to take extra care– can easily be spotted on a night as clear as this" and he could without having to use his torch pick his way down the pathway of gravel to the office, as the moon illuminated the pathway for him.

Reaching the office block, Tony glanced in and as expected found that Tazwinga was already there kitted out in his camouflage uniform. Tony nodded to him and proceeded to his office, unlocked the door and switched on the light.

A smile came to his lips, the police mess had Tilley lamps for illumination, but the Office, thanks to the diesel generator required to run their SSB Radio set, gave out sufficient power to have electric lights in all the offices, plus have a security light from the side of the office which illuminated the prison cell block as well.

Tony had often considered running a wire up from the office, and into the mess, even if only into the lounge, they could then even try and run a television from it- or if not at least a radio- so would not have to keep replacing batteries!

He crossed over to his desk and motioned to Tazwinga, who had followed him in, to take a seat, whilst Tony pulled down the Area Security Map, and without turning asked "Well, Taz, which way do you think is best to go?"

Almost immediately Tazwinga replied" Via Chelenyemba, through to Chief Beyulah's - we could leave the Landrovers there, and proceed on foot from there through to Mambali, sir" he stopped and looked up at Tony.

As usual this most trusted and reliable friend had got it correct - it was almost uncanny how much the two of them always thought in unison. No doubt due to the fact that they had been at Sun Yet Sen from its opening, been through so much together, they had built up a special relationship that was both the envy of many, but sadly too, frowned upon by some of those who still held the racial prejudiced view - some of the latter, sadly, were amongst the very Police Force in which they both so loyally served!

"Fine Taz," Tony replied "go and choose those who will come with us- get them to pick up their rations from the stores- will you pick up mine for me please Taz, then meet me at the armoury - oh- could you also get two drivers and have them to ensure that the two Landrovers are fueled and ready to go, and have them too stand by at the armoury".

"Sir" Taz answered, got up and walked out into the night, and was gone. Tony looked at the security map for a few minutes longer, and then put it away–reaching over he took a photo of his long time girlfriend, Cheryl, from off his desk and held it in his hands looking fondly at it. Memories of their last time together came flooding back.

It was at Gwanda, Gus Armstrong had invited them to a braii (barbecue) being held at the swimming pool.

Now Tony made no excuses for his portly figure and receding hairline - put it down to the hard life he had led–plenty to eat and even more to drink. It was not uncommon for the three of them, Tony, Rod and Dell, to sit on the verandah of an evening, chatting about this and that, and the day's events and before they knew it, they had gone through a crate of beer - that's twenty-four bottles!

And of course since assuming command at Sun Yet Sen, he had become more "chair bound"- gone were the days of his cycle patrols and horse patrols- so he now got less exercise.

Cheryl on the other hand, being thirteen years his junior, had a sylph like figure - which Tony loved - such a small waist, topped off with those ample breasts and that pixie face with those stunning green blue eyes! Her hair she always kept short and styled with that Lisa Minnelli look.

He recalled how he had bought her a new swimming costume for the braii, it was a tiny pink Tanga - one of those that consisted of really just a few triangular pits, of the briefest quantity, just ample to cover the necessary bits!

On their arrival at the swimming pool at Gwanda, they went into the changing rooms to get into their costumes. Outside the "gents" changing rooms, all the single policemen and unattached men from the other various Government Departments at Gwanda, were lolling about. Cheryl got changed and got out before Tony, and he knew precisely when - because from outside the gents' changing room Tony suddenly heard various voices say" GET A LOAD OF THAT!" "Who is she? Haven't seen her before" "BOY - Look at that BIKINI" "Who is she with?" "OOOH I'm in LOVE!"

Tony chuckled to himself and emerged and walked up to Cheryl, took her hand and very slowly, deliberately, strolled passed all the young single lads, over to where Gus and his family were. Tony had on that smug look that said "EAT YOUR HEARTS OUT LADS - SHE IS ALL MINE!"

A little later when he was in the pool itself, he had to carry out a "rescue". It was Cheryl he had to rescue as when she dived in and surfaced, to Tony's surprise he noticed that when the Tanga got wet, it was also "see through" (which would have been all right, if it were just the two of them - but not in front of all these!) so he swam up to her, and after telling her the result of the water on the material, suggested that she should keep below water whilst he got his large towel to drape round her as she got out - but by the look on some of the young lads' faces, they too had got the faintest of glimpses as there was a lot of nudging of each other going on!

Tony recalled that they had given the Tanga to a young girl living and working in Gwanda, and even though they had explained that it was "see through" when wet, she just loved using it around the young single lads, driving them potty - by diving in - getting out and walking slowly passed them, pretending that she was unaware that the costume had gone "see through" just loving the attention and looks on their faces as she did so!

Tony chuckled to himself, as he slipped the photo of Cheryl out of its frame and into his top pocket, then he walked out of his office, switching off the light and locking the door behind him.

As he walked by the Charge Office, Constable Rhodes was still trying desperately to raise Mambali on the radio, but to no avail.

Tony walked on up to the armoury where Tazwinga was already waiting with the assembled crews for both Landrovers that stood fueled and side by side.

All the rations and packs had been picked up and loaded into the trucks.

Rod unlocked the armoury door and started to hand out to each member their necessary FN rifles and ammunition they would require, which each member duly signed for and went and "fell in" in front of the two Landrovers in a straight line.

Many of the wives and children of those African Constables that

34

Tazwinga had chosen, were standing silently, at a distance, watching the procedures unfold before them - no doubt hoping even at this stage that Mambali would answer the calls or failing that, that once their husbands got down to the Mambali post, they would find that once again the duty Constable had just fallen asleep and so would soon be back "home" again - but at the back of their minds, they would have the niggling thought - that maybe- just maybe - it would be worse!

Tony took his keys and chucking them over to Rod said "Take over will you Rod- keep in touch on the VHF set" and without waiting for a reply from Rod, turned towards those waiting and gave them the order they were now anticipating - "EMBUSS" -which had them all scrambling towards and getting into their respective Landrovers.

Once all were in, the engines were turned over and barked into life in the still night air. Lights and VHF Radio sets were turned on and all weapons cocked and safety catches applied - as in the present troubled times one never knew when going out–day or night–when you might come upon a group of terrorists.

Tony in the lead Landrover led the way out of the police camp, as the vehicles trundled down the dirt road towards Chelenyemba Mission, and from there onto Chief Beyulah's kraal and Mambali.

Each and all inside the vehicles, sitting quietly, had their own private thoughts, perhaps not so much of what they were going to find, they had been trained–highly trained especially for occasions such as this, but more so of their respective loved ones and families that were being left behind.

Those loved ones too, would no doubt be harboring the same thoughts, as they stood silently, watching the receding taillights of the two Landrovers in the dark, till they were out of sight, and the final hum of the Landrover engines could no longer be heard in the still of the night.

7

The Shashe River which formed the boundary between Botswana and Rhodesia was, owing to the recent drought only knee to waist deep, as the murky brown water flowed sluggishly by.

During the rainy season this river was a torrent from bank to bank making it impossible and extremely dangerous to try an attempted crossing, even if you were an Olympic swimmer.

It was not uncommon for the rains to fall further up, and a sudden wall of water some four feet high, come rushing down, carrying with it those animals and any humans that had the misfortune of being caught in the middle of the river, even some on the edges too had been swept away by this powerhouse, to their untimely deaths, as the wall of water engulfed them and carried them together with the broken trees and other debris, down to where the Shashe met the great Limpopo River, which it rushed into just south of the Tuli circle. The Limpopo then formed the boundary between South Africa and Rhodesia and continued on past Beitbridge, which was the Immigration post between these two countries.

But now, the Shashe River was no threat at all, as its murky water slowly moved along, lapping over the many boulders and it was easy for anyone, to wade over, and so it was to this, that the band of six emerged from the balancing rocks and shrubbery on the Botswana side.

They were arrayed in an assortment of uniforms, but each carried an AK47 assault rifle, and they paused at the river's edge looking over to the Rhodesian side.

In fact the leader of this gang, had for the past half hour, been surveying the scene in great depth, making sure that there appeared to be no one on the Rhodesian side, before they emerged.

Five of these gang members had been recruited years earlier from within the townships of Bulawayo, and were so chosen not only because of their ability to speak the local language but familiarity with the countryside and therefore would not to be out of place when engaging in conversation with the local Africans in the area.

All were young men who had had their minds filled with the propaganda of the grand promises ahead for them, and as they had all been unemployed at the time, they had been easy targets.

They had all been taken to training camps just a few miles from Lusaka, the capital of Zambia. Once there, they had been put through months of training - their instructors being either Cubans or Chinese, and a few of the more educated Africans from Rhodesia- who had been sent to China for their training and were now back in Zambia putting the new recruits through their training, which was long and tough. But the recruits were regularly fed, had a good supply of beer each night, together with an ample supply of women, regular prostitutes taken from in and around Lusaka, and brought out to them.

So with this, plus the constant teaching of the rewards for "freedom fighters" (as they liked to be called) which was to be the choice of the best housing or farms, plus big cars and managers of companies that they would take from the "white regiments of Ian Smith" had kept them all in service.

The leader of this gang that now contemplated the crossing of the Shashe river into Rhodesia, was himself an ex African policeman from Rhodesia. He had retired from the Force, in fact his last years having been served out in the Sun Yet Sen area, which controlled the area they were about to cross over into, and so he was very familiar with all the local inhabitants, and the lie of the land too.

When he had retired and returned to his homeland, he had been to a beer drink, whereat he had propositioned a woman who had spurned his advances, and he had in a blind fury, pulled out his hunting knife and murdered her.

He had then fled to the Sun Yet Sen area, where he had led the Member In Charge of the Sun Yet Sen police station and his policemen on a merry chase, until they had him virtually trapped, and he had no alternative but to cross over to Botswana, knowing that he could not be followed there by those chasing him - yes it was none other than Ngonga!

Once he had crossed into Botswana, it was merely by accident that he had stumbled upon a terrorist camp, where trained insurgents, such as those that he now led, were waiting to cross into Rhodesia, to wreak their havoc on the local inhabitants in order to intimidate these onto their side.

By this time Ngonga, with no money or food, was another easy target and when he revealed that he was an ex policeman, who knew the area, and in fact the Member In Charge of the police station at Sun Yet Sen - he was given the VIP treatment. He was hustled off to Zambia, and after a brief spell there, off to China for further training and indoctrination. He was a keen student and enjoyed the many "perks" of a life that he had never known, Hotel living, status, plenty of money and fine clothes, but most of all Chinese and European women, and once again he felt that it was his duty to perform, and his tally for women whilst in China rose to great heights and it was with deep sorrow that he was eventually declared ready to return to Zambia, where he became a Senior Instructor and he himself had selected this band, with the sole purpose of crossing, not to harass the locals, but to attack the Mambali police post, then on to the Sear Block post and ultimately to kill Tony–nicknamed NDLOVU - the White Elephant.

The band followed Ngonga into the muddy water of the Shashe, carrying their AK 47 Assault rifles high, with Ngonga keeping a wary eye out, so that they might not be spotted. Negotiating the boulders which had been rubbed smooth by the passing of the waters over the years, they emerged from the river to scramble through the river Combretum bushes, and finally came to rest by and Azanza (snot apple) tree.

Ngonga gave the order for them to rest and immediately posted a guard as the others sat down to eat and rest. Just to reassure himself and also for the sake of his importance he pulled out a map and had a quick glance at it, not that he needed to -the area was so familiar to him and he knew exactly where he was. He nodded to himself as if to say they were in the correct place and folded the map and replaced it into his pocket. The sun was already setting, they looked on fire, and he knew that it would soon be dark, and then their dastardly deeds would begin. "Ah yes" he said to himself "Ndlovu - you so nearly got me before... this time it's my turn to get you."

8

As darkness fell, the Mambali police post went about their duties as usual. The last VHF Radio contact with the "parent" station - Sun Yet Sen had been at 5 o'clock that evening; the next would be due in 10 minutes time.

There was a three man crew, one of which, whose turn it was to be "on duty" for the night, sat at the desk on which the VHF Radio set was situated, drinking tea from his large enamel mug. The second member was asleep in the bedroom area, and the third who had just finished unleashing the police guard dog - a short squat brown and white bulldog who having been unleashed for the night would be free to ramble the whole fenced-in area of the police camp, the main entrance door to the camp, on the fence had been duly locked for the night by this third member of the post, who now came back into the police post, sat down and switched on his portable radio which he tuned into his favorite game show "Pick-a-box" which was sponsored by a leading washing powder company.

These three had been at this post now for the past three months and were due to be relieved and return to Sun Yet Sen In two weeks time. They would spend much of their final two weeks tidying up the police post area and making sure that all the reports that they had dealt with during their tour down at this post, were all "up to date" so that when the Member In Charge of Sun Yet Sen brought down their replacements he would find all as it should be, and it was because of the respect and high regard that they had for him, that they would ensure this to be the case.

Two of the three were single lads the third a married man whose wife and children were also counting the days of his return to Sun Yet Sen. As a result of the "political climate" the country found itself; they would be worried about the safety of their husband and father. Being on a post right on the border with Botswana, knowing that terrorists used this crossing point into Rhodesia, and although no police post or station had come under direct attack from these terrorists, the Constables were at risk whilst on patrol in the area, as they could quite easily come upon a band of terrorists who would count it a feather in their cap to either kill or capture a member of the Police Force, all whom they considered to be in the pay of the "illegal government!"

The Constable themselves were also under some apprehension each time they were posted to either one of the two police posts, Mambali or Sear Block realizing that they could come under attack, but took a lot of comfort from the knowledge, that the majority of the local African populace were not interested in politics, and supported the Police Force, due mainly to the years of positive influence of Member In Charge of the Sun Yen Sen police station had on the area. The Constables also knew that the same man had, and would always "back up" his policeman - yes indeed they drew comfort and strength from the leadership of...NDLOVU...The White Elephant!

As darkness closed in, Ngonga raised those sleeping in his gang. They immediately came too, cocking their weapons and were ready to move in an instant. "This," Ngonga thought to himself, "is why I chose them." They, like the policemen who were willing to follow Tony, were just as willing to follow and die for Ngonga, not only for his leadership qualities, but they had witnessed firsthand his terrible temper, and his bloodthirstiness, as they each recalled his treatment of certain "recruits" who had during their training in Zambia decided that they wished to leave! They shivered as they recalled the slow agonizing deaths of these, who now lay in unmarked graves in the Zambian soil.

Ngonga signaled and they stealthily crept through the thicket of Mopane bushes and the thorns that tugged at their uniforms. The Mopane bushes grew profusely in this area and were the source of the "Mopane Worm" that was actually a large caterpillar which the locals would kill, squeeze out the innards, and then dry in the scorching sun, till they were "crunchy", and they would then eat the remains, as they were a high source of protein - but not to everyone's taste! The bright moonlight supplied by the large full moon showed them easily the way to go, and a sudden "puff" had Ngonga pull up sharply, as a puff adder, trying hard to swallow a large rat, slowly wriggled out of his way. These snakes were the cause for many deaths in the area. They were a slow moving snake, which would not hurry out of the way on the approach of footsteps, and consequently many had stood on them and in return had received a bite, fatal, as its deadly venom pumped into the legs of the victim! Ngonga watched till the snake was out of view, sweat running down his face, he had a dread for these and all snakes in general, and like most Africans too had a hatred for that other slow moving creature, the Chameleon!

Although having spent so many years in the Police Force, he still had a belief in the legend that so many other Africans held, that a large fire was sent to Africa, and God had the Chameleon to warn the inhabitants, but because it moved so slowly, the fire swept through, burning those living in Africa, Who crouched down, palms and feet to the ground - and that is why the Africans, although being different shades of black, their feet and palms of their hands, were white - as Europeans!!!

Ngonga quickly wiped the beads of sweat from his brow and face, not wanting his comrade to see this "fear" after all, he was their fearless leader, the one that would lead these dedicated freedom fighters to great glory and then the ultimate rewards of those high paying jobs, big houses and cars, farms, and then, like their leader they would be able to take any woman that they fancied to be their "bedfellow" for the night - even the "white women" and this thought especially spurred them on to follow Ngonga even more.

It was not long before they had crept up to the fence that surrounded the Mambali police post. Their hearts beat faster as they gazed upon the serene sight of the police post, standing out clearly in the darkening night that crept in over the land.

They could see the shadowy figures against the curtain of the window from the light within, and could hear the laughter coming from the transistor radio, it was a show that they all knew from their time in Rhodesia, it was the "pick-a-box" show - where contestants had to pick a box, and would be offered money against the unseen "prize" inside the box - sometimes it could be a nice prize, other times it could just be a "matchstick", so the contestants had to decide what they wanted - the "money or the box?"

The five wondered just what would be the plan of action this night, knowing that whatever their leader Ngonga asked of them they would respond to their utmost especially since they had been chosen by Ngonga himself, for this mission - a high honor indeed.

The dog on the other side of the security fence that hemmed the Mambali post, was doing its customary patrolling of the area inside the fence, when it suddenly stopped its walking - turning slowly and looking in the direction where the terrorists were hidden from view watching the camp. It very cautiously, with nose twitching as it sniffed the air, started to approach the fence. As it got nearer to the fence, it started a low, deep growl.

That was Ngonga's signal. He had purchased a large piece of meat from the last butchery they had encountered in Botswana, just for this occasion, and whilst the others had been asleep or keeping watch, Ngonga had very carefully "doctored" it–with poison!

Ngonga now tossed this piece of meat from where they were hiding. The meat flew through the night air, over the fence, and landed with a thud onto the ground just a few feet from the dog, which startled, stopped its advance and gave a small quick jump backwards. But then, its eyes, and then its nose detected the tasty looking morsel that had landed close to him, as if manna from heaven - and thinking that all its Christmases had come at once the dog crossed quickly, and wolfed down this tasty morsel, which so very soon cause its death.

Ngonga and the group watched as the dog consumed the meat. Those in the group not knowing that the meat had been laced, by their leader, with poison, thought to themselves how clever their leader was, because now by this gesture, they thought, the dog would befriend them, and they would then be able to gain access and carry out their planned carnage. As they watched, they suddenly saw the dog go into its spasm of death throes, and suddenly realized just what their leader had done, and their admiration for him grew even more. They silently watched till the dog's feet finally twitched no more–it lay still–dead.

Knowing now that there would be no early warning given to those inside, of their impending death, Ngonga brought out the wire cutters, and with expertise- taught to him whilst being trained in China, cut a section in the fence - just large enough for them to crawl through, but so carefully done, so that on their departure they would exit through the same part, and then bind up the section cut, so that outwardly, without careful inspection of the fence, nothing would seem amiss.

Having cut through the section large enough for them to gain entrance, Ngonga signaled the group, who appeared silently from the undergrowth, and crept up to the fence.

Slowly, one by one they squeezed their way through the fence with Ngonga being the last one to pass through- after all he was not stupid- should they suddenly be discovered, being on the outside, he would be able to quickly make his way back into the shrubbery- whereas those on the other side would have to "fight for it"!

Once he was through though- he had them quickly with military proficiency move- three to the back door, three to the front.

Ngonga looked at his watch; it was just coming up to 6pm, when they burst through the front door...

9

The two Constables in the office area at Mambali, were sitting down, each enjoying a mug of strong sweet tea, with a slice of bread, whilst listening to the "pick-a-box-show" on the radio.

The one sitting nearest to the radio from which the show they were listening to was beaming forth, and sitting nearest the door, turned and saw the insurgents burst through the door, and immediately reached over for the shotgun that lay loaded by the office desk, but a short burst from Ngonga's AK47 assault rifle sent three bullets plowing into his head, shattering his skull killing him instantly, and he fell to the floor knocking over the chair he had been sitting on, his enamel mug of half drunk tea clanged down onto the floor spilling its contents, the radio also fell onto the floor and went sliding over towards where Ngonga stood, who brought the butt of his rifle down, with force onto it smashing it into numerous pieces.

The Constable who was sitting at the desk, on which the VHF Radio was situated, and who was about to make his next Scheduled call to Sun Yet Sen, seeing the incidents unfurling before his eyes, reached for the VHF Radio's handset to call for help, when a further burst of rifle fire, from one of the other insurgents sent bullets thudding into his chest, cutting off his cries before they could be uttered, throwing him and his chair up against the wall, his eyes widened as he recognized Ngonga, and as if in slow motion he slipped off his chair and hit the floor with a sickening thud, dying as he did so.

The terrorist who had just shot him, turned his AK47, and fired three or four more rounds into the VHF set- destroying it.

Ngonga, turned - the dark fury could be seen in his eyes as he faced the gang member who had just shot the VHF set. He quickly pulled his .38 Smith and Wesson pistol from its holster, just like a cowboy in a duel, and without batting an eyelid fired two quick shots, which tore into the throat of his "comrade" and up into his head propelling him backwards, and as he fell dying to the floor Ngonga screamed "You Idiot!" for this was not part of the plan, plus he wanted the others to realize the ghastly consequences of their not following his plan "I wanted to hear the parent station calling...I wanted to hear the panic in their voices when they got no reply...Damn!!!" and he turned and stared at the other insurgent in the room.

At the back of the Mambali post, the other three terrorists burst through the back door a split second after hearing the front door being kicked in, and had proceeded to where the third Constable lay sleeping.

At the first sound of gunfire, the Constable awoke and started to get up, only to be roughly grabbed by two of the terrorists, one on each arm, pulling him up from the bed, whilst the third member rammed the butt of his rifle into his stomach, winding him.

They then forcibly dragged him across the floor and eventually through the door leading into the office area where the full effect of the carnage greeted him, and he was immediately violently sick.

His eyes were glazed as he stood there in his underpants, both in fear and horror at the sight of his dead friends, lying where they had fallen in death.

Those holding him lifted him up as a third member stripped him of his underpants, and the two then pulled him over, roughly, to the chair on which the Constable had been sitting listening to the radio show, which the third terrorist had now picked up off the floor and placed in its upright position. The Constable was then pushed down onto the chair, and his legs were spread and bound to the sides of the chair. His arms were pulled to the back of the chair and tied there.

The Constable shuddered as he awaited his fate at the hands of this band of terrorists. As he sat in his naked state, he realised that the one member, who was standing alone with his back towards him was obviously the leader, so peering in his direction he asked "What the hell do you want?"

He recognized Ngonga as soon as he turned and faced him "NGONGA!" he exclaimed, and Ngonga took two steps towards him, right hand raised, and brought his fist down hard on the Constables cheek "ONLY - answer questions that I ask you ....we are not here to indulge in idle chatter" Ngonga responded, then continued "Who is in charge of Sun Yet Sen...is it still NDLOVU? And how many trained anti-terrorist men does he now have?"

As there was no quick reply from the Constable tied to the chair, Ngonga brought down the butt of his rifle, swiftly without warning onto the

Constables left knee, shattering the kneecap with a crunch- and the Constable screamed in agony....then looking Ngonga in the eye replied "Oh YES...Ndlovu is still there" and then with a little laugh, ignoring the pain he was in, continued "You better beware ...you know...he will trample you...just as he has done others like you who have crossed over from your terrorist camps...there is ..NOWHERE, nowhere for you to hide. Ndlovu will ..NEVER, ever forget what you have done here ...you of all people should know that...you are ALL ...as good as dead already" and then as if suddenly aware of his impending death, seemed to give him inner strength, as he continued, now having seen the doubts, and flicker of fear showing on the faces of all but Ngonga, "As to how many trained men he has ...well now ...if YOU ...are only half as clever as you try to make out in front of these followers of yours...then you tell me....I won't tell you anything except this "he paused, for what seemed to be an eternity, till he could see that he now had all their attention, including this time Ngonga, then casually continued," Ndlovu, yes, that White Elephant, ...he WILL get each and every one of you, one by one, till he finally gets you, Ngonga ...you SATAN NYOKO!"

He spat out the last insulting words to Ngonga - who recoiled as though having been hit in the face. Ngonga then pulled out his large hunting knife from its sheath, and swiftly brought it down with one lightning movement, slashing down and cutting off the Constable's manhood, the cut off penis toppling onto the floor as blood gushed out from the severed artery, and then just as quick, he brought the knife up into the helpless Constable's stomach, plunging it in through the skin, up to the hilt, and then withdrew it.

The Constable opened his mouth to scream, one of the insurgents stuffed his mouth with the underpants that they had taken off him earlier, and then they each followed their leader, and spat upon the figure of this dying man.

They then ransacked the police post, taking all the arms and ammunition together with all the foodstuffs that they could find and carry, including the tins of tinned dog food, and then having taken all forms of identity from their dead comrade, including his rifle and ammunition, they quietly left the police post heading back to the cut area in the fence through which they scrambled, with Ngonga once again being the last man through. Once through Ngonga very carefully began fixing up and tying together with strands of wire, securing them tightly. He stepped back and was happy to see that without a careful inspection the fence appeared intact, and with a satisfied look on his face, he too stepped off into the surrounding brush, joining his remaining group, and then in single file they started off towards the Champion Ranch area, leaving a deathly eerie silence behind them at the police post.

Ngonga was now proud of what they had accomplished and having the taste of victory in his mouth, was already planning a similar fate for the Sear Block post, thinking just what this will do for his advancement within the terrorist organization- just imagine, the only person to wipe out, not just one, but two police posts. And now his mind was ticking over, for between these two posts was the white man, Pritzkows ranches, ...oh what a joy if the old man was at one of them, and they could kill him too, his ego was getting bigger and bigger as they headed off, leaving behind the grisly scene that he knew would greet those that would come and investigate why the post had not come up on their scheduled radio calls.

He glanced at his watch, and noticed that it was 7.15pm; their deathly dastardly deed had taken them just an hour and a quarter to accomplish.

"Yebbo, Ndlovu" Ngonga spoke aloud to himself "you are top of my list - may we find an even more agonizing death for you - you white regime trash!" and in his twisted mind he had already begun to formulate different ways that he could think of, that would bring about the worst possible pain, pain inflicted in such a manner that it would take a long agonizing time to bring about death, not only to Tony, but all the others who would see it or hear about it, bringing about the fear of his name NGONGA- yes he would be feared by all the white and African policemen alike, all those like the three they had killed at Mambali, who had been willing to die for this NDLOVU. Yes something to change their minds...to make NGONGA stand out as the MIGHTY ONE. He thought too how the news would travel back through Botswana and to Zambia, and how his name would be held in awe, and fear too, by all the other terrorists.

As they continued through the night, Ngonga suddenly stopped this line of thinking, as reality came upon him once again, and he shivered. Yes shivered again, and he suddenly knew that what that Constable had said was true...Ndlovu, would never give up the chase to catch them, for what had happened at Mambali- he would pursue and pursue, and would only stop when there would be that final confrontation between them, yes just them two...and no matter how much he wanted to recall his previous concepts, and to believe in his own greatness, he had to give way to nagging doubts about the outcome of what he had done...especially based upon what he personally knew about Tony.

Ngonga finally called a halt by a large Baobab tree. The Baobab was like a tree that had been torn out of the earth, and had been upturned, with its large root like branches sticking out. Its large girth truly made it a giant of a tree, and they huddled up against this big tree for the night.

After eating, Ngonga went over to a Buffalo-thorn tree and avoiding the spines at the base of the leafstalk, plucked off the edible fruit it bore, he knew it could also be used like a coffee bean, and so after building a small fire, he put some water into his tin mug, and crushed the beans into this, and once boiled, he supped quietly on his coffee and arranged for the posting of a "watch" arranging reliefs, and then settled down to sleep.

It was the first time that Ngonga had had such a disturbed sleep...such a restless night...made all the worse for his continued nightmare...each time he woke in a sweat from it...on going back to sleep, why, each time, the same nightmare would return...it was the same each time. There he was walking along a riverbank; he went to cross the river, when from out of a thicket a large bull elephant came thundering out at him. He tried to outrun it, but as in all such scenarios he could not run, and was forced up against the bank. The elephant came slowly up to him, then as he cowered down the beast kneeled down upon him, crushing his lower body, and before he could do anything else, the beast suddenly moved its head, and impaled him on one of its tusks!

What a beast of an Elephant...and...yes...this large elephant appeared to be WHITE!!!

Beads of sweat flowed freely from his forehead...he shuddered, as he suddenly realized that this WAS, and could only be....NDLOVU - The White Elephant!

10

Chief Beyulah's kraal consisted of three animal pens, the larger for cattle the next for the sheep and goats and the smallest for the donkeys. As he was a chief, he had built in the center of the kraal area a brick house, with a corrugated iron roof which he and his number one wife occupied. As chief he had also bought for this house, Tilley lamps to provide the lighting in this his main dwelling.

His other three wives and their children occupied separate mud huts with the traditional thatched roofs as did his loyal "security men" and these huts lined the road from the main gate into the chiefs kraal, and they only had the hurricane lamps for the lighting of their respective huts.

The doors as well as the windows of the main brick house were open to get the maximum breeze into the house, and Beyulah had just finished his meal of sadza (ground corn made into a thick porridge) and meat and rape (a green spinach type vegetable) which made up the gravy to eat with the sadza.

Having finished eating he had retired and settled into his favorite chair, a high backed arm chair that Tony had given him some years before. He had only been sitting for a few moments when he lifted his head, and stared out of the doorway down towards the main entrance to the kraal, into the night illuminated by the large silvery moon.

He had heard what had appeared to be the sounds of approaching motor vehicles. "Definitely more than one" he thought to himself, as he slowly got up and walked to the door, where he stood, with his tall slight frame, leaning against the doorframe.

He stroked his grey beard, and then pulling out his pipe, he casually filled it with tobacco, and lit it. Drawing in deep breaths as the tobacco in the pipe caught alight, and the blue-grey wisps of smoke from the pipe bowl twirled upwards, and as Beyulah blew out puffs of smoke, the tobacco fragrance filled the room.

He had been in the doorframe for about ten minutes when from round the corner came the headlights of the approaching vehicles. As he looked his 'security men' came up to his house, and silently stood watching for themselves the approaching vehicles.

Beyulah had already determined that there were two and they were Landrovers, and had concluded that it could only be the police, which had him musing to himself "This could only be trouble...what else would bring two police Landrovers, at this hour of darkness to my kraal?" He stood up erect, framed in the doorway as the Landrovers pulled up before his main house, and he slowly went down the stairs to see what was the reason for these to be coming to him, this night.

*****

The two Landrovers with Tony in the lead one, had on leaving Sun Yet Sen, passed over the newly constructed bridge over the Shashani river, and as they went past the four houses that housed the constructors, Tony noticed that Willem and Pat's car was in their driveway and he felt a pang of guilt.

Willem was the chief constructor, a fine chap from Holland, his wife Pat was a beautiful Rhodesian girl that Willem had married. They and the others had been down here now for some nine months constructing this bridge, which was now practically completed.

Willem and Pat had become very close to Tony, with Tony often inviting them to the police mess for a meal, and thereafter they would settle down to a game of Canasta, and then Willem and Pat often reciprocated the invitation.

It was only after some two months, when Pat started making it quite plain that she "fancied" Tony, making quite an obvious play for him on every occasion she could. She always managed to find some excuse to come up to the police mess to borrow something or other.

It was on one of the occasions that she came up, to find that Tony was on his own - both Rod and Dell being up at Kezi for the night.

To say that she was delighted, would be an understatement "Hi, Tony" she said " I just came to ask if you had any paraffin, I could borrow - I forgot to get some this morning from the store, and we are about out".

Tony sent his batman to get some from the office, and whilst he was gone Pat said "Where are Rod and Dell tonight" and without thinking Tony had replied "they are at Kezi, be back tomorrow", and then suddenly noticed the smile on her beautiful face, and realized his mistake too late, she came onto him in a flash!

49

Now Tony was no prude, but even so, her advances had him gulping. "Willem is away in Bulawayo too" she cooed.

Elliott, Tony's batman, brought in the paraffin, and Tony invited Pat to stay and have a meal with him, which she happily accepted. After Elliott had washed up all the cutlery and crockery he left for the night, and the two of them were left alone, it did not take Pat very long, being the very beautiful woman she was, to worm her way into Tony's bed for the night, and from that moment they had embarked on an ongoing "affair" with Pat becoming more and more brazen, resulting in their very nearly becoming "caught in the act" twice by Rod and Dell, and once by Willem! This continued till such time as Tony met Cheryl, and then cooled towards Pat, and when she finally asked why, he told her about Cheryl. Pat was of course upset, but she still tried to continue the 'affair' stating," Oh yeah Tony, but she is in Bulawayo, and you are here...alone often...and you must, surely miss, not having her here with you...and that's where I can fill the void....no strings attached...just here for each other...what you say?"

Tony thanked her, but declined, saying that they should just continue being good friends, to which she replied "Yeah...that's OK, but...wait...you will see...after a while you will want this 'good friend' to meet your needs!" she laughed, and drove off to her temporary 'home' by the bridge.

The two Landrovers crossed the bridge, passed the Chelenyemba Mission, and had an uneventful drive down the twisting dirt road, towards chief Beyulah's kraal.

As the leading Landrover rounded the corner on its approach to the main entrance to the chief's kraal, and then approached the main house, Tony could make out the figure of the chief, framed in the doorway, and as the Landrovers came up to the house, the chief came down the stairs to meet them.

As the Landrovers drew to a stop, Tony got out and walked over towards the Chief. This elderly statesman, with his graying almost white hair and beard framing his dark brown, wrinkled wizen face, was for his knowledge and wisdom highly respected by Tony.

As Beyulah recognized Tony, he held out his scrawny hand, and grasped Tony's in a firm hold, as they went through the customary handshake - a firm shake, then slipping round the fingers to grasp each other's thumbs, and then back into a shake for a third movement.

"Ndlovu" Beyulah said, using the nickname that he and the others had bestowed upon Tony, spoken in a tone of warmth and deep respect that he had for this trusted police friend, "I'm troubled by your arrival to my home at this hour- and seeing you all in camouflage uniforms, can only suspect that there is trouble again - more terrorists from Botswana I presume "he said and as he paused Tony placing his arm on the old man's shoulder, guided him to one side, where he quickly told him all that they knew, and having finished asked for and attained the chief's permission to leave the two Landrovers at his kraal with the two drivers whilst the rest of them proceeded on foot to the Mambali police post.

Tony had just finished speaking, when a figure came running up towards them from the main gate area up to where the two of them stood. The doors of the huts on either side of the roadway were opened, with inquisitive faces peering out, in some were burning fires in the middle of the huts, in others hurricane lamps were lit, and the light from these shone out onto the roadway illuminating the running figure as he passed each doorway.

Tony and Tazwinga had already had their FN rifles up and aimed as soon as the figure came into view, but as he came nearer and finally drew up before Tony and Beyulah, it was seen that it was Sibanda, One of the chief's headmen, who lived near the Mambali police post.

The man stopped in front of them saying "Nduna, Nkosi" addressing the Chief and Tony, in that order, and then continued "something has taken place at Mambali police post - there were many shots fired - not shotguns like the police have - this was rifle fire - automatic rifle fire, and I think too a pistol, but also...." he paused, and then continued "Oh...so much pained screaming, Babba" he paused looking at his Chief, and Tony.

Tony realized that his worst fears had come about - this was not, as had happened before, a case of the Constables at these posts, having fallen asleep and thus missed their scheduled calls - no this was different. Tony and Beyulah exchanged glances, knowing looks as they both realized that the police post had indeed been attacked, and it seemed no resistance had been offered, so they must have been caught completely by surprise "Where the hell was the dog?" Tony thought to himself, then remembering the headman's words of pained screaming that had been heard, Tony well knew the barbaric tortures that the terrorists employed, and he felt a shiver as he stood there in the night- but this shiver was not due to any cold night air.

Tony turned and found that Tazwinga had already got the Constables out, formed up ready to go.

Tony approached them and simply said " This is no drill, lads - this is the real thing again - except this time, it does appear that they have attacked our police post- so be prepared - they could be anywhere by now- so watch yourselves as we go " and with that he crossed over to the lead Landrover, picking up the VHF radio receiver, he called the Sun Yet Sen police station, Rod was still up, Tony spoke to him, telling him what he knew so far- and told Rod to radio in to Gwanda and to let the Officer Commanding know.

He then grabbed his pack, and after leaving instructions with the two drivers that were remaining with the Landrovers at the chief's kraal, shook Beyulah's hand once again. "Humbagashle" (go with care) his old friend said to him, and at Tony's signal, with Tazwinga beside him, they all left at a sedately trot, the line of camouflaged men being picked up as the crossed the light coming from the open doorways of the huts, and went towards the main entrance, and then they were out of sight, into the darkened night - not even visible in the moonlight.

Beyulah then had his own "security" men, who were allowed to be armed with shotguns and placed them on alert too, for as a chief, loyal to the Rhodesian Government, he too was a prime target for terrorists, and it certainly seemed that this group of terrorists were just not intent on intimidating the locals, but having attacked a police post, then he knew that this group was not the "normal" that had so far crossed over from Botswana, and so the Chief sent runners to the other chiefs and headmen in the area to forewarn them too, and only once he was satisfied with the "security" arrangements for his kraal, did the old wise man once again retire back into his main house.

He once again sank down into his armchair, staring up at the wall where he had in place a framed picture of the Prime Minister of Rhodesia, Ian Smith, and he began to wonder just what lay ahead for this fine country, that was experiencing these unprovoked attacks by mindless people, who had been so brainwashed by those who were hungry for change and power. Beyulah knew from the example of countries to the north of them that those who had gained their so called independence soon suffered from mismanagement, bribery and corruption. "Why can't they leave well alone" he mused to himself, as he puffed on his pipe, and pondered the future.

11

Tony, Tazwinga and the Constables, travelling is single file, continued in the moonlight, on their trek towards Mambali, this lowland area, and poor grass cover, especially in the 'drought' was the ideal growing area for the Ebony trees, which grew in abundance, together with the Acacia and Baobab, and Mopane in this area.

As they pushed through some sickle bushes and approached the Mambali police post, Tony had them all fan out and take cover in the undergrowth - for they did not know if the terrorists would still be in the police post, or if they had already gone.

The moonlight clearly showed up the police post - there were no outwardly signs that anything was amiss- the main gate still appeared locked, and there was no structural damage to the building, there was only a deathly hush.

After observing the scene for some time, and seeing no movements from within, Tony and Tazwinga cautiously slid out from the nearby bushes, FN Rifles in their arms they crawled on their stomachs up to the main gate of the security fence that surrounded this camp. Reaching this, they lay for a few moments listening, but hearing nothing but the distant baying jackal. Tony whispered to Tazwinga "Cover me Taz" and then he slowly raised himself up and examined the lock on the gate, and noticing that is was unbroken, still locked, he crouched down again, and then the two of them crawled back to the relative safety of the shrubbery and joined the others.

After instructing them to "cover" the building, and for one to be the "rearguard" watching should anyone come up from behind them, he and Tazwinga started a slow walk through the shrubbery as they traversed the fence, being aware that they could come upon an ambush at any moment - so they moved with as little noise as possible, trying not to step on too many dry twigs and leaves.

As they came to the last stretch of the fence, that led up to where they had left the others, Tony suddenly stopped and motioned to Tazwinga who immediately came up alongside him. Tony pointed, and Tazwinga could see, in the moonlight lying on the other side of the fence was the police dog, which they could tell from the fact that there was no movement at all, that the dog was not asleep, but dead. "That's why they were caught" Tony thought to himself "no advanced warning" and he felt a twinge of regret, for he particularly liked that pug ugly squat bulldog, and recalled how the dog used to like to bite onto a tyre that hung from a tree in the yard, and how once it had locked its jaws onto the tyre, Tony could swing the tyre high, up and down like a swing, and the dog would just hang on in there!

They started to move on, and had gone but a few yards when Tazwinga pulled up, so suddenly, that Tony almost fell over him. Tazwinga crouched down low, and then beckoned Tony over beside him and pointed to the fence.

Tony bent low and looked keenly to where Tazwinga was pointing, and as he did so, he noticed what Tazwinga had seen. Barely visible, he could make out where the fence had been cut, and then expertly bound up again with strands of wire, which had been trimmed down so no untidy tell tale bits could be seen - nothing appearing to be out of the ordinary. "Cleverly done" Tazwinga whispered, and Tony nodded in agreement adding "Well spotted Taz- must be them carrots you have been eating" he joked.

Looking down into the fine sand and dust by the fence, they could see in the moonlight, that the area had also been swept, so that any marks at this point could not be easily seen, but a few yards from the fence, just before the shrubbery started, they could see the unmistaken boot prints, of the type used by the majority of terrorists, and this was again confirmation that there had definitely been activity here, and Tony wondered what lay inside. Were all the Constables killed, or had they been captured? Were the terrorists still inside the police post, waiting for them to come - waiting for them to come up to that front gate, and gain entrance, or had they left already?

They rejoined the others in the group, and then Tony had them follow back to the site of the cut fence. Slowly unpicking the wire strands, they opened the cut in the fence, and then slowly - one by one - they crawled through.

Tony had chosen this method of entry, as he thought that should the terrorists still be inside, the last place they would expect anyone to come in through, would be the place where they themselves had come in from.

Once inside they crawled slowly on, circling the camp, being prepared for a firefight, their rifles trained on the building.

Tony reached the front door with Tazwinga behind him. They both took a deep breath, nodded to each other, and then Tony slowly reached up for the door handle. He motioned that he would go in high, Tazwinga low, once Tazwinga had nodded agreement, he slowly pushed the door handle down, as the door started to swing open they both dived in.

The ghastly sight that met their eyes, made them freeze! The bloody carnage was everywhere. There under the table, by which the shattered VHF radio set was located, was one dead Constable. The other lay spread across the floor by the side of his smashed transistor radio, and alongside him was the dead terrorist "Good" thought Tony "they got one of the bastards", but as Tony turned the dead terrorist over he could see that this one had not been shot with a shotgun, which the Constables had "Mores the pity" he mused to himself, thinking how it would have given some satisfaction if they had managed to get at least one. "Well, well" he murmured "I wonder what he did that his leader did not approve of...eh...Taz?" He did not want or expect an answer. As the other anti terrorist group approached, Tony had them surround the camp and take up whatever cover they could find, and keep a watch out towards the bushes in case this was still all part of a trap.

He and Tazwinga now focused on the third member who was in the chair, his underpants still stuffed in his mouth, his eyes wide open. His manhood lay by one the legs of the chair on which he was tied to, and the vicious stab wound was quite obvious "The Bastards" Tony hissed, as he leant over and started to undo the rope, to free the Constable from the chair.

Tazwinga helped him, and they lay the Constable down on the floor, then went into the bedroom, returning later with blankets, into which Tony and Tazwinga placed the bodies of the three dead policemen, and lay them side by side on the floor.

He and Tazwinga then did a quick recce of the post and could see that all the shotguns together with ammunition had all been taken, as had all the tins of dog food "Boy they must be damn hungry - to want to eat that!" Tony thought to himself. They noticed that there was no other food in the camp so presumed that what there was had also been taken by the insurgents.

Having completed their recce, and as the VHF set had been shot-up, and therefore no longer serviceable, Tony had Tazwinga call up the "radio man" who came up quickly to them. Tony contacted the Sun Yet Sen station, and asked Rod to pass on to the Officer Commanding at Gwanda the sad news of what had happened, to also contact the dead Constables relatives, on his behalf and inform them too, ensuring that they be made aware that Tony would not rest till he had caught up with those responsible. That was his promise.

Tony ended by saying that he would be getting one of the Landrovers from Beyulah's kraal, to come down and pick up the dead bodies and transport them back to Sun Yet Sen - and that they then would be going after those responsible, once they had retained the services of the tracker - Goliath.

Goliath, so called because he was so small was a Botswana bushman, who lived just inside the Botswana area, but who had become Tony's tracker. They first met, when Tony had hunted for antelope to provide meat, not only for the police station, but also for the Prison staff and prisoners at Sun Yet Sen.

Tony recalled how Goliath, (the name that Tony had given the bushman, because he found it easier to pronounce than his real name) - had shown Tony the art of tracking.

Tony had always marvelled at what Goliath could "pick-up" from nothing that could be seen, be it a bent twig on a bush, or a leaf that had been trod on, and could tell Tony what direction the animal they were tracking had taken.

He also remembered how he had been hunting with Goliath on one occasion when they had come across a herd of Elephants. Goliath had stripped off his old tattered vest and skin trunks, and then crossing over to a still steaming mound of elephant droppings, picked up some and commenced to rub his body with it, paying particular attention to under his armpits, and round his genital areas, and he then approached the herd walking within arms distance of them! The Elephants had been cautious of him, but scenting only their own "droppings" paid no more attention to him. Goliath had returned to where Tony was standing, and had asked Tony to join him in this venture, and although Tony had been highly impressed, he had on that occasion declined the offer!!

Goliath had gone on to inform Tony, that to be good at hunting, the art was not to be detected. He said too, the same with hunting terrorists, that he should not at any time, use things like toothpaste, or soap to wash with, and certainly no aftershave or body deodorants, for the smells of these could be carried on the wind, and detected not only by animals, but also those, like the terrorists that did not use such implements, and thus give them an advanced warning of the presence of "intruders".

So bearing this in mind, once the terrorist activity had commenced, Tony had ensured that all his anti-terrorist trained men were all made aware of this - and when called upon, one of the first things that they did, prior to changing into their camouflage uniforms, was to have a shower - without soap, and wash off thoroughly any trace of soaps and deodorants that they may have used. Also, all the time that they were out on any "sortie" they would use none of these, in so doing they too would not be able to give any advanced warnings to those they hunted.

Tony had asked Tazwinga to dispatch one of the Constables to cross the Shashe River, and proceed into Botswana to where Goliath lived, and bring him back, as they certainly would be needing the services of this fine tracker.

After about fifteen minutes they returned. The small bronze coloured man came trotting up, his craggy face lit up in a wide grin exposing pearly white teeth- that grin he always seemed to have, no matter what situation, it was as if to his "tracking" was the highlight of his life!

Tony and Tazwinga soon filled in Goliath as to what had taken place, Goliath shaking his head and "tut-tutting" as they did so, and then they took him to the spot where they and the terrorists had gained access, and once through it took only a few moments, and a few steps into the bushes, before Goliath excitedly held up his hand, fingers spread wide apart, to indicate that there were five men in the group they were after, and pointing half right indicated the way they had taken.

Tony marvelled once again, how this little bushman could have found out so quickly this information, using only the moonlight to assist him!

Tony had Tazwinga leave four Constables behind at Mambali to guard the camp and wait for the Landrover to come to remove the bodies, and then signalled the others, and they joined Goliath outside the fence.

Goliath came over to Tony and said" Come- Ndlovu - they are only a couple of hours ahead of us - but we WILL catch them, this I promise you Ndlovu- then they will pay for what they have done here tonight "and with that he went into his crouched tracking stance, and proceeded to lead them out, picking their way slowly through the moonlight night, silently through the bushes, trees and undergrowth.

Goliath was able to notice the slightest disturbance of soil, twigs and leaves that showed which way the terrorists had taken. He had well read in Tony's eyes that Tony could not rest till he had caught those responsible for what had happened at the Mambali police post.

He had been Tony's tracker, not only on hunting trips which the two of them had always enjoyed, hunting not for the sport of it, but for the reason hunting should be done, to provide meat to eat - but had also on many past engagements against terrorist groups - been the tracker that had led Tony, and even the army, to find, capture and destroy the bands of terrorists that had crossed over to Rhodesia from Botswana.

Yes he knew that Ndlovu- The White Elephant, would not stop till he had in fact "trampled" those who had carried out this dastardly deed!

As they pushed forward through the brushes and Mopane trees, they disturbed a genet which was eating a young spring hare it had caught.

Tony recalled how he and others used to take the Landrover out onto the old airfield at night. With one member driving, another using the spotlight, and the third member seated in the spare tyre which was on the bonnet of the Landrover, they would drive round the airfield till they spotted a spring hare and give chase to it.

The spring hare would bound along, hopping like a kangaroo on its large back legs, its two shorter legs held in front of its chest. The chasers would get as close as possible to it, trying to avoid running it over - then the member whose turn it was to be seated on the tyre, would jump off, and rodeo fashion, have to try and catch and hold down the spring hare - being careful not to be run over himself! Once successfully caught, he would signal the others in the Landrover, who would draw up alongside, and the Spring Hare would then be released - but its capture noted in favor of the catcher- then they would swap positions, and the whole procedure would then re-start. The whole idea was to see - who by the end of each month- would hold the record of MOST CATCHES!!

Tony's memories were cut short, by the sudden halting of the group. They had come upon a stony kopje, and Goliath had stopped them whilst he went slowly on all fours, clambering over the kopje looking for signs, even on this stony ground, that would give an indication as to which way the terrorist group had gone.

For what seemed like ages but in actuality had been only minutes, Goliath returned once again - his face in a wide grin "No trouble - Ndlovu" he smilingly said "they went up and over to the left "chuckling to himself, as pleased as punch that he had found the way they had gone, and how little trouble it had been to do so, and he continued "there is a nice cave over to the right - which they missed-stupid ones - it would be a perfect place for us to rest up for the night " and on seeing the look on Tony's face - knowing that his friend did not really want to stop- he went on to say "do not worry- Ndlovu we can continue again, at first light in the morning they will not get far from us." Tony saw his wisdom - a little sleep would do them all some good, so indicating to Goliath to go on, they followed the little man into the small, but adequate spaced cave, and there they settled for the night, with Tazwinga arranging for guards to be posted, and reliefs to be made during the rest of the night - so that all got a fair share of what little sleep there was to be had.

They broke out their rations and shared a meal together, talking in hushed whispered tones, before finally settling down for the night.

Bats that had been disturbed, flew in and out squeaking noisily at the intrusion, but eventually they too settled down, when realizing the intruders intended no harm to them, and happily shared their accommodation with these unwanted guests!

Tony rolled out his kaross (a blanket made from animal skins- sewn together) and was soon asleep, but being a light sleeper, at the changing of each guard, even the slightest speaking had him wake for an instant, then nod off again once he had seen what it was that had woken him, and ensured that all was in order.

12

Before the first rays of light even peaked over the distant horizon, as the very first hint of light started to top the sky at the horizons edge, Tony woke up, sitting up with his back against the cave wall. The Constable who was on watch approached and asked "Shall I make a fire - so we can have some tea-sir?" Tony knew that the Constable, having had anti-terrorist training, was not talking about a literal brush fire that would smoke, and thus give away their position, but was rather talking about the small primus cooker that they carried, for such occasions.

"Thank you - yes - that would be nice "Tony replied, and it was not long after that he was able to sup on a strong cup of tea.

As he did so, Tony started to smile to himself as he thought back to a previous "sortie" in which they were chasing a band of Terrorists. He and five others who formed the "killing group" were to form the "killing line" up on the edge of the Shashe River, onto which the gang of terrorists was hopefully being driven. On reaching the river, they saw on the other side of the river on the Botswana side, a nice outcrop of balancing rocks which would make an ideal hiding spot, and from where the terrorists would least expect them to be. Knowing that this would be breaking the rules – since they were not supposed to cross the border - so to speak - Tony and one of the other Section Officers, Koes, decided to go ahead anyway - and so as it became dark, they crossed and set themselves up amongst the rocks, which formed a perfect look-out position. They decided that if the terrorists were seen crossing the river, they would wait till they had climbed onto the bank on the Botswana side, just in front of them, when they would then open fire, and after killing them, drag them back quickly to the Rhodesian side!

So after posting a watch they settled down. The time was late June, the winter months in Rhodesia, and being right on the river's edge, it was colder than usual.

It was so cold that by the time it was Tony's turn to stand watch - the cold finally got the better of him. He started to browse around, and crawl about collecting as many small dry twigs, old leaves and tufts of dry grass that he could find, which he put in the center of the group of bodies that were lying asleep. Quietly then, he looked around for some bigger twigs, and also found some old dry rotting logs, which made a nice assorted bundle of kindling. He reached into his pocket, pulled out a box of matches, and lit a small bundle of twigs and tuft of grass- blowing slowly onto the flame, and the grass immediately burst into flames, which in turn caught the twigs and finally the logs, soon there was a roaring fire in the circle of sleeping bodies. Koes woke up and said "What the hell are you doing Tony?" Tony had replied "Keeping warm". "What a damn fine idea" Koes responded "well if the swine come over and catch us - at least we will die nice and warm!" and at that moment the others woke up, and were soon all huddling round the lovely fire. As it was the terrorist, had backed tracked, and had gone further upstream towards Plumtree, the railway crossing point from Rhodesia into Botswana where they had run into an Army Patrol and some had been captured - others killed, so really no damage was done by their breaking the rules!

Sitting up against the cave wall waiting for the dawn to break, Tony had time to reflect on how he had actually come to join the Police Force.

He had actually been working as an indoors salesman for a Pharmaceutical Company in Salisbury (the Capital of Rhodesia), the lady in accounts, had a nice daughter who Tony started to take out. It was on his first invite to her house for dinner, that he had met her father, who was an Assistant Commissioner, in the B.S.A. Police Force.

After dinner he had asked Tony if he had ever considered joining the Police Force, stressing the attractions of an outdoor life - especially after hearing about Tony's upbringing in the bush of Kenya, and so soon got Tony's interest aroused, so that he arranged for Tony to meet him the following day, during his lunch break, and he would take Tony up to meet the recruiting Officer.

The following day as arranged, he duly arrived, picked Tony up and took him to the Police Headquarters in Jacaranda Avenue - so named because the whole of the avenues was lined, both sides, by Jacaranda trees - which in bloom with their purple flowers, were quite a sight to behold.

Tony followed the Assistant Commissioner from his official car. Tony was attired in his best suit, clean white shirt and tie, and as they approached the Constable on duty at the front door came smartly to attention, flicking out a finely executed salute, as Mr. Harries -the Assistant Commissioner and Tony passed him by. "Oh, I like that" Tony mused to himself, as it gave him an air of importance.

They climbed the stairs and walked down the corridor, till they reached the door, which had a sign outside saying "Recruitment Officer". Mr. Harries knocked, and walked in.

Inside the recruiting officer, Superintendent Lem Tuke, was sitting at his desk. As Mr. Harries entered, Mr. Tuke, rose smartly to his feet. Mr. Harries explained why he was there, saying "Aaah, Mr. Tuke, like you to meet my good friend, Tony Wood, who would dearly like to join the Police Force- would you assist him to do all the necessary" and without really waiting for a reply turned to Tony and said "I will leave you in the capable hands of Mr. Tuke - when you are finished, my office is third down the corridor, on the left- come and see me, and I will run you back again" and with that left the office.

Mr. Tuke, fussed about Tony, making sure that he had everything that he needed to fill in the necessary form, making arrangements for a medical, whilst Tony did so.

Tony smiled to himself as he went on to remember how during his six month training course at the police depot, how on one of the afternoon parades, which was usually taken by the Depot Chief Instructor, Chief Inspector Trangmar - a man who with the eyes of a hawk could detect specific movement from so far away and had a clear voice that would carry over the green square, and easily be heard by all on parade "You there ...that man...second squad, middle row, third from the right...STAND STILL - you horrible little man." This would cause the one who was fidgeting, to squirm, because he knew that when it came to the Inspection, he was responsible for causing his squad, to be the one, that the DCI would inspect himself!

On one occasion though, Tony recalled that the DCI arrived for the inspection accompanied by Recruiting Officer, Mr. Tuke, and they chose the squad that Tony was in to inspect.

Tony's heart sank, for that day of all days, his batman, had whilst ironing his starched shorts, had managed to put a burn mark down the side, just in front of the right hand side pocket, of the khaki shorts.

Tony was in the middle row, and as the inspection proceeded he tried to move his right hand, with clenched fist in the "attention position" ever so slightly forward so as to cover the burn mark.

As the DCI and Lem Tuke approached, they moved from the person on Tony's right, the DCI giving Tony a brisk look before slowly going towards the next person on Tony's left. Lem Tuke though, paused, spotting the burn mark that Tony was trying hard to conceal, and stopping, took his leather officers cane, and slowly began to push Tony's hand backwards so the full extent of the burn was revealed. "Well - what" he started to say- which caused the DCI to stop his inspection of the person on Tony's left, and to swing round and start to come back towards Tony "Oh, hell" Tony thought to himself "I've had it now - another night behind guard" when suddenly Mr. Tuke looked up at Tony, and he must have suddenly remembered how it was Mr. Harries the Assistant Commissioner who had brought Tony to him, and for a second, his mouth was open but no words came out, the look of anger he had on his face was suddenly replaced by a smile, and he went on "er- what do you think of the training, then lad...enjoying it?" and Tony sighed a sigh of relief and answered him, and the inspection proceeded.

Years later, he and the then Chief Superintendent, Lem Tuke had been on the same train, as they journeyed from Salisbury to Bulawayo, when the two of them had reminisced over the incident, and they both enjoyed a laugh as they recalled the incident.

Tony had often been asked by parents of young lads his opinion of their sons joining the Police Force, and he was always to highly recommend this. The six months training was excellent way of drilling respect into a young man's life, for those in authority, and it also built into them a feeling of comradeship. Once they had passed out of the training period, then the aspects of being in a Police Force, which up to the year of 1960, had never fired a round in anger, what a fine reputation indeed! Tony always remembered with pride his being part of the "review" parade that was held for their Honorary Commissioner, Her Majesty the Queen, the Queen Mother. How proud he felt as he marched onto the police Square, to join the other squads assembled, from all the different types of "police life" that were gathered, to the applause of the great crowd that had gathered to witness the event. How the Queen Mum, had boarded an open backed Landrover to review all those on parade, she being slowly driven by, whilst the police band played appropriately the "Elizabeth Serenade" and Tony was sure that as she passed by she actually smiled at him! And of course the whole proceedings, of all assembled was controlled by that booming voice, of the DCI, Trangmar.

Getting back to the training - he had always stressed that any who joined, had to be the sort that would be able to take the "shouting and screaming" of the Squad Instructors in their stride - not to take it personally or let it get them down- rather to let it wash over your head.

Some could take it, others would let it get to them, and that caused them deep distress, and would often lead them to either "buy themselves out" or even to desert, or as one did, commit suicide!

But enduring it all, you could always look back and see the funny side of it all, even though it did not appear funny at the time. Like on one occasion, during the early morning PE, whilst running across the common, they came to the pistol range. The squad instructor had the squad halt, and form up into two "sides" of seven, this was made easier, as there were seven in the squad from England, the other seven being locals or from Kenya and South Africa.

Having got the two sides, the instructor had them form a human ladder, and the teams had to see which would be the first to get all members over the brick wall, that formed the backdrop to the pistol range.

The "ladder" was formed using the heaviest-thickest set member, at the bottom, one on his shoulders, a third on top, then the others would use these, to scramble up and over the wall. The last one up, would lean back over, before jumping down, and pull the top person of the ladder up, who in turn would just be able to pull then next person over, and finally that just left the two bottom members, alone, trying to reason out, how the heck they were going to be able to get up and over this brick wall, without any help from anyone. So they looked for, and managed to put to use, various "holes" cut out from the wall from where the bullets hit, and using these, were both able to pull themselves up a few feet, but then, there they were stuck. No matter how much the instructor hurled abuse at them, there was no way up, the instructor knew this, and eventually stopped his screaming, and they all fell in, and continued their run. As they passed a dump, the squad was called to a halt. The instructor went over to the dump, and after poking about for a while, re-emerged with two old, rusty, dirt encrusted "chamber pots", he handed one to Tony, and the other to the other team member with the instructions, that they had to present these to the DCI, at the afternoon inspection–GLEAMING!

There was also the occasion, when taking a break during a "foot drill" lesson, that the Instructor, used to pick at random, a squad member, to come forward and give a talk on any chosen subject for three minutes - if the unfortunate man was unable to do so, he had to run round the square, holding his rifle above his head- Tony was once called upon, to give the three minute talk, on - A BUBBLE!!! Needless to say, he had to make the 'run' with Rifle held high over his head!!!

Then of course there was the Stable parade- the cleaning of the horses, during which time one of the squad members, had walked behind the horse that he was "grooming" when it kicked out, both barrels (feet), hitting the member in the chest, knocking him over, where he collapsed in a heap. Tony and two others had started to rush to his aid, when the instructor had yelled "AS YOU WERE -- get back to what you were doing - leave him be" and then coming up to the horse and where the downed member was, looked at him on the ground and continued "Do hope that you did not hurt my precious horses hooves- poor animal!" and spent time examining the horse, before returning to see if the squad member was all right!

All these were the Instructors way, that you as a trainee had to try, and not let get to you. So too the room inspections, when you had to have your bedding and uniforms laid out "just so" and make sure that there was no dust on any ledges- for the inspecting instructor, would run his fingers over the ledges, and examine the bedding and uniform layout with eagled eye precision, and if anything was amiss, then the offender would be, for sure, behind guard that night!! But it was all deemed necessary part of the training, to see if you could "take it".

Tony recalled that when he left for his posting from the depot, how he had waved "good-bye" to all that "bull" only to find that on getting to Gwanda, the then Member In Charge, who had just been promoted from Chief Inspector to Superintendent, had introduced Friday Mornings as Inspection day! They had to "fall in", after having their uniforms they were wearing inspected- they were given some "arms drill" followed by a room inspection- and although they did not have to have their bedding and uniforms laid out as in Depot whilst training- the rooms had to be neat and tidy- and once again dust free ledges. "Oh, no, "Tony had thought when arriving there, "It's like being back at the depot"!

The first calls of a dove, brought Tony back to reality. He noticed that the sky was slowly lighting up, as the sun started to rise over the distant horizon, its bright orange rays, peaking over the hill tops, whilst down by stream edges, fog patches slowly disappeared. He folded his kaross, and put it back into his pack. The others in the group also awoke, had a cup of tea, and it was not too long before once again they were, on the spoor of the terrorist gang, with Goliath as usual leading the way, as they jogged off down from the kopje, from the cave where they had spent the night, and into the shrubbery.

13

Bison Pritzkow was a short squat man with silvery hair, his skin a dark tan from constantly being out in the sun as he patrolled his ranches. He owned the Nazeby, Nazeby South and Champion Ranches, that lay to the south of Sun Yet Sen, with both the Nazeby South and the Champion Ranches, bordering onto the Shashe River. Along with his cattle, on these ranches there were herds of elephants, zebra, impala and wildebeests, with also lion, leopard, hyena, jackals and other small antelope, for Bison loved the wild life, and only hunted for the pot.

He was as tough as old boots, and much preferred to ride his horses when checking his ranches, rather than use his Landrover. He always said that there were two reasons for doing so, the first being that the horse could get to parts on the ranch easier than the Landrover could, and in fact could get some places where the Landrover could not get through at all, and secondly because a horse could not be heard going through the trees etc, whereas a Landrover could be heard from miles away, so there was more chance, if there were poachers on the ranch, of him being able to come upon them on horseback rather than when in his Landrover.

Bison and Tony had struck up a friendship and mutual respect, going back to the days when Tony was in charge of the Stock Theft Section, and Bison had been plagued with the Theft of cattle from his ranches. Tony had come down and camped on the Champion ranch, for two months, staying in the corrugated iron building that Bison had erected on the Ranch, using this as his Headquarters for his investigations.

It was here too that Tony first met Goliath, the wiry little bushman, and they too had soon built up a rapport, with Goliath acting as Tony's tracker, when hunting to provide meat for the pot, and for the making of Biltong (meat from an antelope, cut into strips, salted and peppered, and hung out to dry- which once dry could be eaten and was delicious! Especially if you had a Lion or Castle Lager to go with it!)

Through his investigations, Tony finally arrested and subsequently got convictions against fourteen accused persons, but not only that, he had also managed to bring about the recovery of nearly half of the stolen cattle - the other half having been slaughtered. All of this of course endeared him to Bison, and they had become firm friends.

Bison and his "mistress" Mrs. Day had been delighted when the Sun Yet Sen police station had been built, knowing that they would at last have a police station nearby which was a comfort, but they were even more so when they heard that Tony was to be the Member In Charge of this police station.

Once Tony had arrived, it had become a regular thing for him to be invited down to the Nazeby Ranch, every Monday and Friday evenings

There with Bison and Mrs. Day, they would sit on the verandah, each having their own favorite "tipple" as the sun sank over the horizon, watching the last red fiery colours in the sky disappear. Then Bison would go and start up his diesel generator, which supplied the house with electricity.

It would not be long before the house servant would come and inform them that dinner was ready. There was always a soup, followed by a main course of either a roast, or stew and dumplings, but always - there was the same desert, it was Tony's favourite desert - large thin pancakes, filled with slices of banana and syrup, surrounded with a lot of fresh cream, and a half lemon to squeeze over it all!

Having eaten they would retire to the lounge, where after a cup of percolated coffee, they would pull up their chairs round the log fire, and with a glass of fine brandy, they would sip and chat about the past, and listen again to many a tale of Bison's wild experiences, especially from his early days on the Ranches. On the Friday evenings, they would all sit round a table, and enjoy a game of Canasta. The Nazeby Ranch house had all the mod-cons, and not at all like the house at Nazeby South, which with its thatched roof, was lovely to look at, but like Sun Yet Sen mess, only had Tilley and Hurricane lamps for lighting purposes.

Tony had on one occasion been down at Nazeby South, with Bison, sitting in the lounge, after dinner when there was a loud "plop" as a puff adder snake fell from the thatched roof- there being no ceiling- just broad beams, and landed on the floor- where it lay for a few moments, before being chased by Bison into the garden. Tony always shuddered to think what might have happened if the snake had fallen onto one of them...it did not bear thinking about.

Sleeping at night, did not trouble him, as there was always the mosquito nets, which they had, and that would prevent anything from falling upon you whilst you were sleeping- so at least you could go to sleep without worrying about a snake crawling into the bed with you!

14

Bison emerged from the main building at Nazeby, walking together with Mrs. Day, in deep conversation, as they headed towards the gate leading out from the gardens, onto the gravel road, on the other side of which were the garages and stables.

He bade Mrs. Day farewell and walked briskly over to the stables and saddled his favorite horse, a "grey" which stood some fourteen hands high.

He had already phoned through to the Nazeby South Ranch, and informed them that he was coming, and would be there for a week, whilst the dipping of the cattle was done.

This was something that had to, by law, be done on a regular basis, to keep the ticks (a blood sucking parasite) off the cattle, for each type of tick could carry a different type of disease.

There was always a large stock of provisions at Nazeby South, and Bison's trusted cook, an old grey-headed man, by the name of Toby, was known for the most delicious meals he served. Toby's wife kept the ranch house spotless, taking pride in doing so, referring to it as "my house" - whilst her son was in charge of the gardens, and also tended to the vegetable patch to ensure that there was always an abundance of fresh vegetables on hand, and that too Toby's son took pride in doing.

Bison together with his two herdsmen, also on horseback, left Nazeby and headed south. They did not follow the dirt road, that ran between the two ranches, with Bison preferring whilst on horseback, to ride the direct route, through the large expanse of wooded land, over the hills, and through the dense foliage, he like Tony, had a love of the open spaces, and so enjoyed this trip to Nazeby South and Champion Ranches. Bison–like Tony revelled in, being one with nature, and only ever hunted to provide meat for the pot, as it were. He enjoyed the actual tracking of his prey, and then as soon as he had shot an antelope, usually an impala, he would rush up to it, slit its throat and then disembowel it, leaving that spoil to the jackals, or hyena's and of course the odd vultures to fight over, and then take the rest back to his ranch.

On the Champion Ranch there was a fine specimen of a Kudu Bull (a large antelope) with its fine curved horns that nearly everyone wanted to "bag" as a trophy.

Bison recalled how he and Tony had been out hunting together one time, and as they stepped out of the bushes onto an old dirt track, there right before them stood this fine old Kudu bull. Tony, who had handed his rifle to his batman to carry, signaled quickly for it, and for what seemed an age, they stood looking up at this fine animal, which stood its ground majestically, looking back at them.

When Tony had got his rifle, he looked at Bison, shook his head, and Bison shouted "Go–you fine hunk–go back to your herd of females–you're too good to shoot" Tony slapped the butt of his rifle hard, and with that the Kudu bull turned, and with a magnificent leap, bounded into the thicket and out of sight, and both Bison and Tony were glad that neither of them could bring themselves to shoot it.

Bison remembered how they had gone on only a little while when they came across a herd of Impala, Tony had raised his rifle and fired, both he and Tony could hear the unmistaken "thud" as the bullet struck the animal that Tony was aiming at, and the herd immediately sprang off - all except one - which stayed, standing quite still. Tony whispered "That's the one I aimed at - cheeky devil" as he re-loaded, and shot again. Again there was the thud as the bullet struck home, and the animal remained upright where it was. Puzzled they crept closer, and closer, and when the animal remained routed to the spot, they eventually had crept right upon it, and then they noticed, that both shots had entered the beasts spine within an inch of each other, and had completely paralyzed the animal - thus why it had not run away, or why it had not fallen, and how Tony had been upset in having "wasted a bullet!"

As Bison and two herdsmen rode through the land, they passed herds of impala as well as herds of wildebeests and zebra - which always seemed to graze together, and the only acknowledgment these gave to the three riders, was to stop their grazing for a few minutes, as the male impala's "snorted" loudly, their ears twitching, tails wagging, as they watched the riders pass by, and then returned to their grazing.

They came to the Shashani River, which was a tributary of the Shashe river, and formed the boundary between the Nazeby and Nazeby South ranches, and which ran southwards also forming the boundary between the Nazeby South and Champion ranches, which too owing to the drought was only a trickle, of water.

Bison remembered how on one occasion, he had left his Landrover on the side of the river whilst he took his dogs into the middle deepest part of the river, where after drinking they jumped in and swam downstream, with Bison following along on the side.

It was the rainy season, and way upstream, in fact in the Matobo and Kezi area's they had had a real downpour, a violent storm with heavy rain. The result of which, was that all the drainage from these areas, all the little streams from all the rocky Matobo area were suddenly full to overflowing, and all of these ran into the Shashani River, which by the time it reached the Kezi area, was bank to bank, a raging torrent of water. With what it picked up from the Kezi area as well, the Shashani River, swelled to disastrous proportions, and what was just a slow flowing river, now had a wall of water sweeping down.

The next thing that Bison knew was the crashing sound" and as he looked up he froze for a moment, as he saw, tumbling towards him down the river came a wall of water several feet high. He managed to scramble up the bank, with his dogs right at his heels, just in time, but alas his Landrover, which he had left upstream, was caught in the wall of water, and was tossed about and carried along, as if it were a paper toy, and was later found some five miles downstream, wedged amongst some low lying trees!

The three horsemen, crossed the river and proceeded down to Nazeby South, arriving late in the afternoon, and Toby as always had lit a fire under the 44 gallon drum, that was filled with water, and was the source of the hot water supply, so that on his arrival Bison was able to enjoy his usual long hot soak in the bath, after his ride down.

The following day, Bison had spent over at the Champion ranch, rounding up and then supervising the dipping of the cattle, and returned once again to Nazeby South, late in the afternoon.

After his bath, he had a fine meal of roast guinea fowl, with all the trimmings, after which he had had a coffee, and then walked out onto the verandah to get some fresh air. The evening air was something that he loved. No "fumes of pollution" here, from either factories or vehicles.

No here in the evenings, with all the vast covering of trees, bushes and shrubbery all around, there was only the quiet clean air. The chirping of crickets, hooting of a spotted eagle owl, and of course in the distance the baying of jackals, only interrupted by the occasional clanging, of pots and cutlery and crockery as Toby and his wife, washed and dried up those used for the evening meal.

Bison just loved this solitude, it was part of his routine, to stand and take in this evening air before eventually retiring to bed, and this evening was to be no different...so he thought!

He always kept strapped to his side, cowboy style his colt 45. He also kept in his arms cabinet, a FN Rifle, loaded, in case of trouble, together with his rifle, and a shotgun - for he realized that in the present unsettled political climate, that the country found itself in, nothing could be taken for granted anymore!.

"Those good old days are gone" he said to himself, as he stared into the night, and at the age of 70 years, he was right. The days when the only danger he encountered was from wild animals, a wounded lion or leopard - were long over. Oh, yes, there were still wild animals, lions, leopards and elephants too, on the ranches, but now, the dangers no longer came from these, no now it was dangers from man... or rather a certain type of man...one that had its head filled with the promises of taking over any "white man's" ranch that they wanted once they had won, what was described to them as their "freedom".

Yes sadly now, it was now danger from these terrorists that one had to watch out for...and the sad thing was that they never stopped to ask how you felt, or take the time to find out how you treated your African staff, no as far as they were concerned, if you were "white" and had Africans working for you, well that made you enemy number one...and if to boot, you were also a rancher...well that made it "open season" and you were definitely one that had to be erased!

"What a sad situation" Bison thought to himself," what on earth is going to happen to this fine country–as if it was not enough, having to overcome the sanctions that the British Government had imposed, they now also had to be prepared to face the possibility of meeting up with a group of these terrorists, who had adopted the name, and were in fact viewed by many countries worldwide who were now anti Rhodesia, "freedom fighters". "FREEDOM - freedom from what?" Bison asked himself, for give them any name you want to, it still boiled down to the fact that they were, and would always be, Terrorists. Bison sighed, and sadly shook his old wise head, and turned to go back into the house.

15

Ngonga woke in the early hours of the morning, just before the sun rose. He was drenched in sweat - sweat not due to any heat - but due to the recurring nightmare that he had had once again all night. Even now it was vivid in his mind, he had been trapped against a bank by a large bull elephant...but as always this elephant was almost white in appearance!

Ngonga now soaked, shivered... "NDLOVU" he hissed... for he knew well enough who the elephant in the nightmare represented, it was none other than his once Member In Charge, the one that had organized his farewell party for him on his leaving the Police Force. The one who had presented him, not only with a new cycle, but that fine plaque with the BSAP Badge, a fine lion, with a spear in it, with other spears and a shield under it, and under it a banner in three segments, with the words which read "PRO REGE, PRO LEGE, PRO PATRIA" - and how happy he had been to receive this from Tony, for whom he had had such a high regard- he had always viewed Tony in a different light to so many other European policemen many of whom still regarded themselves "superior" purely by the colour of their skins - many of the new Patrol Officers, just out from their training - considering themselves superior to the African Constables, regardless of how long the African Constable had been in service, some even considering themselves more superior to even the African Sergeants and Sergeant Majors who had had over 20 years service - yet Tony was different.

He was sad too at having to leave the "esprit de core", the comradeship with many others he had lived and worked with.

He remembered that when he had murdered that woman, at the beer drink at his homeland, how he had fled to the Sun Yet Sen area, as he knew it well, and how he had always managed to keep just one step ahead of Tony - who was pursuing him, sometimes only just managing to give him the slip, till finally he was driven across the border into Botswana. And it was only during this period that he had started to take a delight in being able to outfox his old Member In Charge, and it was then that, he started to form a "hating" for the one that he once had admiration for, for he knew that this man was after him, to arrest him, and try him, and have him sent to jail...and in his mind he knew he could not face that, and so he started to dislike Tony, and began to take joy, at eluding capture.

Once he crossed the border into Botswana, everything else happened so quickly, his meeting with the terrorists in Botswana, then his journey to Zambia and the large camp many with young lads taken from 'raids' into Rhodesia and many young girls also taken captive, and now used solely for the enjoyment of all those in the camp, and then his being spotted as potential leadership leading to his being sent to China for further training, and he could recall his fine time in China, especially the fine time he had with many a Chinese and other 'ladies' laid on for his 'pleasure' and how he had enjoyed even more the use of these oriental and white women, and the old familiar stirrings in his loins became prominent again, and he had to shake his head to clear his thoughts..."Time for more of that when I complete this mission" he mused to himself. Bringing his thoughts back to his present situation and how his life had taken such a drastic U-turn, which now put him in opposition to Tony–Ndlovu. He shivered once more, as he recalled the nightmare. He jumped up, reaching for his canteen, opened it and poured some of the water over his head, not only to try and wake him from this nightmare, but also, so he could if asked, account for the wetness on his uniform, not wanting any of his group to know that he had been in a sweat from the nightmare or his carnal thoughts!!!

When the sun eventually rose over the horizon, Ngonga woke up the other members of his group; they all sat down and had some bully beef, and after burying the empty tins, set off in the early light towards the Nazeby South ranch. From there they would be able to cross to the Champion ranch, and from there on to attack the Sear Block police post, and from there, he could see them actually going on to Sun Yet Sen, releasing the prisoners who would he was sure be on his side, and with the extra arms and ammunition from Mambali and Sear Block, they would easily be able to overcome any resistance from those at Sun Yet Sen - and Oh, how such acts as these that he was figuring out in his warped mind, would raise his esteem, not only within the Organization he belonged to, but also among the Cubans and Chinese...and aaah, how much more, he would be able to demand, and get, the attention of the "white women" for whom he had now got a "taste for"! All these grand thoughts were running through his mind, and he had to stop and bring himself back to reality once more!

It was no doubt that by now, someone from the Sun Yet Sen police station, would have been down to the Mambali post, and the report of the carnage would have been related back to Tony at Sun Yet Sen, who would by now be sending out his trained ant-terrorist squad, to try and find those responsible- or at least which way they had gone...and that's why he had led his group onto and over that kopje, for even if they had managed to track them up as far as that, it would take some time for them to skirt the whole kopje area, to find out and pick up their trail once again...so there was no need to be in a great rush. They had to keep to the bush though, for it would be obvious in their uniforms, that they would be recognized as terrorists, and Ngonga knew that Ndlovu - enjoyed the privilege of a host of informers - these too...would soon be wiped out, as they too were regarded as traitors to the freedom cause!

So confident was he, that he failed in his most fundamental tactic, to keep a "back-watch", and so was unaware that already Goliath was on their trail, and had on one occasion already seen them in the distance, pointing this out silently with hand signals to Tony, which only he and Tony understood, and Tony's heart had leapt, with the satisfaction of knowing that they were now closing in on this murderous band.

Ngonga pressed on at a leisurely pace, throughout the day, constantly stopping for him and his group to drink, or to relieve themselves. As dusk fell, they came upon some Marula trees, and decided to settle there for the night.

The Marula trees bore fruit which when ripe fell to the ground and fermented, and in fact became a potent alcohol, and many a funny scene had been witnessed of Elephants and Baboons, who had eaten a lot of these fermented fruit, getting quite "tiddly" and their behavior being hilarious to watch.

Ngonga now so confident that he was so ahead of any chasing forces, committed the second unforgivable mistake, this time it was allowing a fire to be lit, on which they boiled water to make a strong brew of tea, and heated up the tins of dog food, which they had taken from Mambali, which they quite happily ate! Either they could not read that it was dog food, or that they did not care!

After having eaten they all settled down for a sound night's sleep- all that is except Ngonga, who once again found his mind overcome with the previous nights nightmare, which returned to haunt him yet again, resulting in his having very little sleep, what little he did manage to snatch, was so upsetting that he found himself once again shivering and in a cold sweat. No matter how hard he tried to think of different things, even the biggest thing in his life, which was women and sex, even those could not eliminate the nightmare from his mind. He tossed and turned, and then sat up, hugging his knees to his chest, and then putting extra logs onto the fire, he got up and walked into the bushes to relieve himself, after which he returned, and once again tried to catch some sleep, but it was constantly interrupted by his nightmare.

16

Tony and his trained anti terrorist squad, had come across where Ngonga had spent the previous night, and thanks to Goliath had located where they had in fact buried their bully beef tins in the sand. They continued to follow the wiry little bushman, Goliath as he led them on through the day, zigzagging, and cleverly picking up the terrorists spoor, even on the areas of hard baked ground, without letup, closing the gap between them, and finally came to rest that evening, happy in the knowledge that they could be no further than approximately three quarters of an hour behind them.

Goliath found an old deserted donkey kraal, and they made use of this for the night, again taking turns to stand guard, so that all could enjoy a measure of good sleep, after having an evening meal.

It was about two hours after they had eaten, that Goliath, made his way over to where Tony was lying down, and gently tapping him, motioned to Tony to follow him. Tony got up and followed behind Goliath. They had gone a few yards past the Constable on duty, when Goliath stopped.

He lifted his head high, and sniffed, Tony did the same, and suddenly it came to him, the unmistaken smell, of a wood fire. Goliath grinned, in the moonlight his pearly white teeth shining up like beacons, and he pointed over to the left, of where they were camped, the direction from which the night air was blowing, bringing the smoke from the fire that the terrorists had made to them "How careless" Tony thought to himself "someone slipped up, or did they not know that there would be someone on their tail so soon" either way, it was even more of a comfort to know that they were that close, and after tapping Goliath on the shoulder, the two of them ambled back to join the others and settled down for the night.

The following day, again rising early Ngonga who had had little sleep, woke the others, and after having something to eat and drink, they hastily kicked sand over the fire that had been kept going all night, and then proceeded to go on their way once more.

It was approaching midday as they topped the rise of a hill, and Ngonga called a halt to let himself and any of the others relieve themselves. When Ngonga had finished, and returned to the hill top from a clump of bushes, he casually strolled about with an air of importance, and it was only by chance, rather than by design, that he just happened to look back from whence they had come.

Through the bushes, Ngonga suddenly noticed a line of figures, moving quickly but silently, and suddenly he froze. "No... surely not" he mused to himself "can't be a chasing group - how would they have been able to catch up so fast." Deep down inside, he knew that ordinary folk from around the area would not be moving the way they were moving, that would be what you would expect from an army or specially trained group of men.

He quickly fished out his binoculars, and then raising these to his eyes, not thinking of whether the sun would glint off the glass or not, he adjusted the focus, and then looked once more in the direction he had seen the movement.

He caught his breath–when through a clearing, came a wiry little bushman, who Ngonga instantly recognized "It's Goliath" he hissed, he knew all about this little bushman's prowess for tracking, and knew now how this group had been able to catch up so easily - but also he knew that this little bushman tracker, was a good friend of Tony's, and as he continued looking, behind the bushman into the clearing, was the unmistakable figure of his one time Member In Charge, of the Sun Yet Sen police station, yes it was - Ndlovu! He shuddered, as the memory of his recent nightmares came back to him, which he quickly dismissed, and then smiling to himself said "But, you were not able to catch me before, and you won't again." He raised himself and calling his band members together, informed them of the chasing group and urged them onto a quicker speed, he did not want to be caught up in a battle here - not before he could achieve his aim, and they scurried on down the other side of the hill, being more diligent now, keeping a constant back-watch.

It was late afternoon when the terrorist band came across a kraal that bounded onto the Nazeby South ranch. As they approached the kraal, the kraal head recognized Ngonga and called out a greeting to him and started to walk out to meet him, when he suddenly noticed the others emerging from the undergrowth - and realized that Ngonga was not in the usual camouflage uniform used by the police, and that the arms they carried, were similar to those carried by the terrorists of which his chief, Beyulah had informed and warned him about.

He froze, and called out to his wives and children to remain indoors and to lock the doors to their respective huts.

Ngonga, seeing that he and his gang had been recognized, ran up to the kraal head, and smashed the butt of his rifle into the old man's stomach, which had the old man doubling over in pain as he collapsed to the ground. Two of the terrorists grabbed hold of him and hauled him back up onto his feet.

Ngonga turned to him with a large grin and said "Hey- Ndaba - what's this? I come to see you - yet you tell your family to close their doors to us ... is this the way you greet and treat an old friend?"

Ndaba had not yet properly caught his breath, so he just stared at Ngonga, seeing in Ngonga's eyes, behind the smiling face, a dark, sinister side, which made his blood run cold.

Ngonga continued "Come...now...tell your wives and children that we only want some refreshment, and to fill our canteens -it's hot and we have travelled far...so...go old one...tell them to open the doors for us" those last words came out, not as a request, but more as an order, and Ndaba knew that some evil intent was about to happen.

But he was in a catch twenty two situation.

Due to the circumstances that Rhodesia found themselves, anyone found to be "harbouring" terrorists was arrested. This was an area where Tony's view differed from others, and many a heated dispute had taken part, when Tony had tried to get others to put themselves in the situation. "Think about it "Tony had often said "Your house is invaded by terrorists...who demand to be fed. Now to fail to do so, could, and in most cases would, mean getting killed, if not you, then certainly your loved ones...so what would you do? Feed them? BUT, if you do, and are found out as having done so....what happens? You are arrested and imprisoned! Think about it!" Yes it was a question that many had to think about. It was a completely different picture if those who gave succor, were know sympathizers, then yes Tony could understand the arresting and imprisonment, but when it was some terrified family, who did so out of fear for their lives...then he could not understand - to be sure the law was an ass!

This was the situation that Ndaba found himself in. He tried to reason with Ngonga "Ngonga...Babba...you know that it has been a long hard dry year...what little water that we have...we have to get from the nearest borehole...which is half a day's walk from here...so what we have here is only sufficient to last us from the setting of the sun, till it rises next morning...for you are aware... once it is dark, it is not safe anymore..." he stopped suddenly realising that he had now touched a raw nerve, as Ngonga's smile faded, and he shouted " YOU...in the huts...Open up and bring us water...NOW! Do not try my patience" and as he finished he brought his foot up and kicked the door of the nearest hut to him, and inside the cries of fear from small children could be heard, as they huddled together- in fear at the final outcome of this confrontation.

From somewhere, Ndaba gained the strength to shout "NO...don't open doors - it will end in sadness "and his words were cut short, as Ngonga turned, and with a savage blow to the face, which landed on and broke the old man's nose. As the blood flowed freely from his nose, Ndaba sank once again to his knees. As he did so, one of the other terrorists, who had been holding him, kicked him savagely in his kidney area, knocking him onto his face, into the dust and dirt, which clung to the blood flowing down his face.

Those in the huts could hear what was happening, and the senior wife, who had been peering through cracks in the hut walls, knew too that if they resisted any longer, the gang could, and would kill her husband, but would anyway force open the doors, and take what they wanted, and then possibly kill them too.

So to put this all to and end, she hoped, she shouted "Ngonga...no more I beg you...let him be...I am going to open the doors and bring water to you" and she slowly opened the door, and then signaled to her eldest three daughters, who were also in the hut with her, who were aged thirteen, fifteen and seventeen, to bring out what little water they had.

As they emerged they could see the pitiful figure of their father lying on the ground. The senior wife, ran up to him, squatting down and turned him slowly over, giving a low gasp as she saw his bloodied face, and cradled his head on her lap, tears running down her cheeks.

Her three daughters obediently carried out the water, and Ngonga said "See...how all of this could have been so unnecessary...if only your husband had not been so stubborn." He then turned to the gang members and told them to fill their canteens, which they did, and as they did touched the three girls inappropriately. This made all three of the girls squirm and cry in alarm as they withdrew from these unwelcome advances.

Ngonga seeing their plight, instead of coming to their aid, his sexual appetite had him saying to the other gang members "They are a fine catch eh? Very ripe and young...take your time with them...it might be a long time before you get the chance again" he was interrupted by the senior wife's plea "Ngonga- No...no, tell your men to not take the children, here, I and my two junior wives, will take their places...those are but children" but her pleas fell on deaf ears, as the gang who had paused waiting further instructions looked over at Ngonga, who said "No...go ahead...take the children...it will be a lesson for those who do not willingly give us what we ask for...go... pleasure yourselves" and as he said that the group grabbed the three young girls and carried them, roughly, screaming, into the huts and started to tear the clothes from their young bodies, as the girls continued screaming, they hit them knocking them to the ground, in a state of collapse, where they continued to rip off their clothes till they were all naked, they laughed and then set about raping the three helpless cowering, girls whose cries again filled the air, whilst the fourth member stood outside listening and chuckling to himself.

Ngonga stood, looking on, quite unconcerned, but then given his appetite for women, that would be just about right, in fact he already had stirrings in his groins, as he was vividly picturing the goings on inside the hut.

The three gang members, raped the three girls repeatedly, the fourth member then went in, and picking out the youngest girl did the same to her as well.

As if that was not enough of an ordeal for these three young girls, when the fourth member left, Ngonga now entered. He went into the hut, and then set about, raping all three in turn. As Ngonga came out re arranging his clothes, the whimpering noises from the three young girls filled the air. Ndaba who the other terrorists had forgotten all about, got to his feet enraged at what had befallen his daughters, and took a dive at Ngonga, who although was not expecting this sudden attack, was far too quick for the older man, and grabbed his rifle, and brought it down upon the old man's head, knocking him out, and he tumbled and fell in a heap and lay still.

Quick as a flash, Ngonga sprang on top of the old man, pulling his lower lip out, he once again produced his large hunting knife, that he had already used on two prior occasions with such horrific results, and with it proceeded to sever the lower lip off from the man's face, and threw this over to the senior wife saying "Now...cook this...and eat it....IF you wish to live...and don't want us to kill you all!"

Although appalled at this, the senior wife knew, to fail this time, meant certain death at the hands of this madman, and she slowly walked over to the kitchen hut, wherein sat the other two wives, with looks of horror on their faces, and tears running down their cheeks, as the senior wife, now got a pot, and placing the lip in it, placed it over onto the fire. It resembled a swollen caterpillar, as it began to sizzle in the pot.

Ngonga entered, and stood there watching as she cooked it, and once it had been cooked, the first wife, duly withdrew this, and very carefully, amid tears streaming down her face, she passed it between her lips, and slowly started to eat it, retching as she did so.

Ngonga walked out, signaled the others, and they left - leaving behind them the weeping and wailing and mayhem, which carried on the air, till they were out of earshot.

Feeling more "cocky" now, not at only what had just transpired, but also for the fact that they had managed to stay ahead of Ndlovu, for yet another day, Ngonga congratulated himself, as they pressed on towards the Nazeby South Ranch house.

17

The police group led by Goliath, had been trailing the terrorist gang, since getting up that morning, and as Goliath came out of the thicket, into a clearing, he was suddenly aware that there was on the hill up ahead, a sudden glow of reflected light- the sun had caught something and had reflected right in his direction, as Tony was right behind, he quickly silently signaled, and Tony, without breaking his stride, gradually lifted his head, and saw it too, a distinctive bright reflected light, once twice, up on the hill - someone was watching them - without realizing that by doing so, they had given away their position. They carried on, uninterrupted, with Goliath and Tony, both being forced on by this last incident knowing that what they had seen was for sure Ngonga and his aides watching them, and he said to himself "Yes...Ngonga, I hope you saw us, specially me...and you would now know that THIS time, I will not let you slip away,...this time you will surely pay dearly for what you did!" He gestured to the others following him, to increase their pace, as they headed to the hill. Goliath had already seen exactly which way they had taken and before they knew it they were over the hill and down the other side.

They arrived at Ndaba's kraal, about half an hour after Ngonga had finally left. The women were still in a state of shock, and were weeping and wailing.

The senior wife re-told the events as it happened, and Constable Katemu – Tony's "first aider" did as much as he could for Ndaba, whilst he got onto the radio to Sun Yet Sen.

Del informed him that the first Landrover had brought the bodies back from Mambali, and Tony asked him to send the second Landrover, to come and pick up Ndaba and take him to the Chelenyemba Mission Hospital, where he knew that Major Munn and her Hospital staff would care for him. Del also told Tony that Gus Armstrong had been in touch, and had both Army and Air force on standby, should Tony require them.

Tony told Dell to thank Gus for this, but to assure him, that he and his group would be able to complete this task as a purely police action and bring down those who had killed their comrades at Mambali, and by so doing redeem, the memory of them.

18

Bison stood for a few minutes breathing in the cool evening air, Toby as usual had cooked a lovely meal, and Bison was now enjoying his customary few moments of quiet time, taking in the serenity, listening to the night noises, that he loved , the solitude to reflect on either the day's events, and to recall the past or ponder what the future would hold.

Across from where Bison stood, was the concrete water tower, holding the water supply to the ranch house, and on the side of that was the steel windmill, that pumped the water up from the borehole, and it was to these that Ngonga and his band now cautiously approached.

Ngonga knew the ranch well; he knew that at most times it was only the staff that was there, although at times, he knew that Mr. Pritzkow also stayed over. The thought of Mr. Pritzkow being at the ranch did not trouble Ngonga, for he knew that Mr. Pritzkow was an old man, and therefore would be no trouble to overcome - should he have to do that - but up to this point he had not included in his plans the possibility of coming across Mr. Pritzkow, or what to do if he did - but already as he thought about it, he did in fact welcome the chance, of coming across the old "white man", for he would kill him too, so that his reputation would even be more enhanced.

Ngonga was slowly circling the water tower, with these thought running through his mind, when he came to a sudden stop. He raised his hand, so that those following him also stopped. Looking across the space between the water tower and the house, there was the squat figure of old man Pritzkow, taking in the evening air.

He noticed that the old man, had with him - in fact he remembered that even during his police days, all he ever saw the old man with, was that pistol , strapped to his side- cowboy fashion - never ever saw any other weapon, and so concluded that that this old man only had the pistol as his only weapon." What a push over " he thought to himself "Like taking candy from a baby" and already he was imagining that with the killing of this old man, he would become the new owner of the Ranches.

83

As Bison turned, Ngonga raised his rifle, aiming it at the old man - "Die you old white trash" he whispered coarsely as he squeezed the trigger.

As he did so, Bison bent over - the crack of the AK 47 rifle sounded, and the bullet, which had been aimed at the old man's chest, struck him in the top of his left arm.

The force of it, together with the momentum of his bending over, lifted the old man, and threw him back against the doorway, and he toppled over into the living room.

Toby, hearing the shot, without hesitation ran to the weapons box, unlocked it and pulled out the fully loaded FN automatic rifle, and the pump action Shotgun - Toby having been thoroughly instructed in the use of the Shotgun, and ran with these towards the living room.

Toby's wife and son, who had been in the kitchen, at the sound of the shot, immediately put into action the well rehearsed plan that Bison had taught them. They locked the Kitchen door, doused the light in the kitchen, and then ran down the corridor, turning out the lights in the bedrooms, dining room and living room, before returning and hiding under the dining room table.

Bison had withdrawn his pistol as he fell into the living room, but had not as yet fired a shot- "Let them think they have got me" he whispered to Toby, as his trusted friend handed over the FN rifle to him, "Leave the door open "he said, as he crawled up behind the sofa and settled down to wait further developments. He was grateful that his wound was but a flesh wound, clean through, no broken bones. Toby had open the medical box, and with his help Bison managed to apply a pad and bandage over the wound, and although it must have pained him, Bison did not show in his face that it did.

Ngonga having seen old man Pritzkow knocked over and thrown back into the living room, and no cries or shots being returned, said "YES ...so will die all the whites...we will have their lands" then turning to the others, feeling very proud of his achievement of having, so he thought, killed his first white-man–and how easy it was to do so. "Come, let's go and see what we can take from here" he said to his contemporaries, and they started to edge slowly towards the house.

The full moon clearly showed them the way as they crossed over the neatly kept garden. Ngonga had noticed the lights go out in the kitchen and bedrooms, but when suddenly the lights in the dining room and the living room also went off, he fell to the ground–the others in the group doing likewise. "Go to the back, and try the kitchen door" he instructed the two gang members nearest to him, who immediately began crawling along on their stomachs, moving towards the rear of the house.

Ngonga suddenly thought to himself that old man's servant does not know that I have left the Police Force so he called out- "TOBY - it's me - Constable Ngonga - I heard a shot - I came as quick as I could - is everything all right old man?"

Toby had in fact, been well kept up to date with events, and had been told by his employer, Bison, about Ngonga's retirement, his subsequent murdering a woman and fleeing to Botswana, and realized Ngonga's trick, he went along with it. "I too, heard the shot - Ngonga - Mr. Pritzkow is dead, I am afraid and have put all the lights out" he called back.

Ngonga felt really puffed up with pride, his immediate plan was working out. He retorted "Toby - Come on out- I am over on the lawn - just down from the water tower" but Toby called back "No - I am afraid - afraid that whoever fired that shot may still be out there - I am scared they might kill me and my family too - I will stay in the house till I am sure that they have gone."

Ngonga thought for a moment "Damn stupid man ...still...he does still think I am a policeman...so that is good" he mumbled to himself, then he signalled to one of his gang members, brought him up close, and told him to go into the house, calling out "OK, wait in there, old friend - I am coming in to join you - then we can work out what to do...do you hear me Toby?" he asked. "Yes" replied Toby, and Bison turned and looking at his trusted servant said "Well done, Toby, I'm in your debt ...now get under cover by the armchair, and cover the passage area, in case any come in through the Kitchen" and Bison impervious of the pain from his left shoulder, lined up his FN rifle covering the doorway, through which earlier he had come toppling through. "Come on - you Dogs of War" he muttered to himself "I may be old, but a lot tougher than you think, and by golly, before you get me, I will take out as many of you as I possibly can "as he checked his rifle, it had as Tony had told him, a double cartridge case, one, strapped to the other upside down, so that when one case was empty, you ejected it, turned it over and inserted the other, no need to fumble about getting bullets out to reload the case and re insert it.

As he settled down, he heard the kitchen door being kicked at, and eventually burst open. Then Ngonga's voice again "Toby...can you see me, here I come towards the doorway" he said as he pushed his comrade forward.

The gang member came walking forwards, Ngonga fell flat to the ground behind him, as he walked onto the verandah, and slowly approached the door.

Bison waited, he could see in the moonlight the shape of a person, holding a weapon, mount the steps onto the verandah, and slowly approach the doorway, he waited, wanting to be sure of his shot, as Toby called out "YES! I see you Ngonga, come in quick. Come inside and join me, before you too are shot." That was all that the terrorist wanted to hear, he chuckled to himself as he thought how clever a plan his leader had thought up, and just how stupid this old man was in believing it, and his step quickened as he entered the doorway.

Bison waited, heart pounding in his ears with excitement, till the shadowy figure filled the doorframe, then sent a burst of fire into the body. The body of the terrorist, taking the full force of the FN rifles bullets as they tore through his clothes, skin, sinew and bones, lifting him off his feet, flinging him backwards, back onto the verandah, as he reeled back his finger squeezing the trigger of his AK 47 rifle, sending a flurry of shots into the roof, as he screamed a muffled scream, as blood pumped up into his throat, and he died.

Ngonga was stunned. He had been outwitted by Toby...that frail old grey-headed, white man's servant...this would not look good to his gang members, and others should the story ever be told, but then he suddenly became aware too, that that was no pistol shots he had heard, that was a FN Rifle...his blood ran cold...NDLOVU!

Had Ndlovu beaten him to this ranch house and been waiting for him? His mind raced, it was in turmoil - surely not...yet again that would cover up for his being fooled - yes it could have been Ndlovu, telling Toby what to say...but could he have known that we would come here? He was really mixed up, and could not think clearly for a minute.

As he was thinking, the kitchen door was kicked in, and one of the terrorists, on hearing the shooting taking place, came running down the corridor towards the living room.

Toby waited...and as the terrorist appeared Toby fired two shots in quick succession, which sent two 3A rounds, point blank into the terrorists face, taking most of it away, as he was hurled backwards, blood, and skin splattering all over the walls, and with a dying scream, his twitching throes, had him squeeze the trigger of his rifle, and shots tore harmlessly into the floor and walls ricocheting through the living room. The second man waiting at the door, at seeing this, ran blindly, scrambling his way back towards the water tower.

Ngonga still gathering his troubled thoughts heard the shotgun blasts, and now, was really worried, for he knew that the African policemen were also armed with shotguns, and again his fear overcame him....perhaps Ndlovu had beaten him to the ranch house after all, and was in fact waiting for...but...if that were so...where were the rest of his chasing group?

He had to try and control his sudden fear....and get his thoughts back into shape...things were not turning out quite as he had expected. He signaled to the other member, near him, and together they started to withdraw, back to the relative safety of the water tower, where they encountered the third member, who informed Ngonga that the other one who was with him, died in the house.

"Damn" Ngonga exclaimed, noting that now they were only down to three - "We will set up here - take whatever cover you can - we will wait and see what Ndlovu is planning "he said, and the other two who were with him, exchanged glances - this was the first that they had been told that this "Ndlovu" was in fact here - and seeing their comrades killed, and themselves down to just three, now began to think, that this would indeed be the time, to think about, leaving this ranch and returning to the safety of Botswana, to regroup and get together with some more members.

Ngonga, sat and began to think, just what they could do, and it was only after a few minutes that he suddenly said "YES - I've got you Ndlovu" as he remembered that he and the others still had their hand grenades, "Huh - we will blow you up, or out, and then kill you" he said, and straight away his courage returned, he would formulate a plan, and win a fine victory here at the Nazeby Ranch South, that would be talked about for years to come!

Tony, Goliath and Tazwinga were leading the "chase group" with Goliath still doing his customary splendid tracking, even in the dark as they followed the spoor of the terrorist gang, taking comfort in the fact that they were gaining on them all the time, faster in fact that they had expected. Tony and Tazwinga, as well as the others, had been dumbfounded, when Ndaba's wife had told them that the leader of this gang was in fact, that ex policeman, Ngonga.

Ngonga had been one of Tony's best African policemen. A brilliant investigator, but alas, just could not put down on paper, the brilliant head knowledge that he had, so after sitting for promotion and failing, had remained as a Constable, not bothering to try and sit the exam again, but for that was a valued member of the Police Force, whose ability was respected by all who came across him.

And it was for this reason, that Tony could not understand, how, so shortly after retiring from the Force, he could have committed the murder of that young woman, and to find out now that he was in fact a terrorist leader, but not only that, but how could this ex policeman, now come back, and carry out the barbaric murder of those members at Mambali, all of whom he knew and worked with, his ex fellow police members - and then to carry out the Mutilation of Ndaba, and the excessive rape of those three young girls...just how bad had this man become - had he lost all sense of rightness? Surely, his confidence could not be that high as to even begin to think, that he could get away scot-free from all of this!

Tony's thoughts were interrupted by the unmistaken sound of an AK 47 Rifle shot. The whole chasing group came to a halt. Goliath called Tony and Tazwinga over, "Nazeby South Ranch house–Nkosi" he said, and now Tony's mind, began to race - "Were they attacking Toby - that frail old man and his family - or was Bison there too?"

He signalled to Goliath, and said "Lead on–let's go and see what's happening, before they kill yet more innocents," and with that they set off immediately at a swifter run than before, off towards the Ranch house.

They suddenly heard a burst of FN rifle fire "Aaahh - Bison is there "Tony mused to himself, knowing that this old hardy man, would give as good as he got, but even so, an extra stride was put into their pace, this was speeded up yet again, when they heard the two blasts from a shotgun, and more AK rifle fire. "They are putting up a fight" Tazwinga said, as they all broke into a run...heading straight for the Nazeby South ranch house! They were all hoping that they would be there in time, to help those in the house, and of course to kill those who were attacking it.

19

The telephone's continuous ringing finally woke Cheryl. She reached over sleepily, and took it off its hook, and mumbled "Hello," not being fully awake.

It was Rod on the other end. Tony had given him instructions, that should the Mambali episode turn out to be a "contact", and if he and the group were to go after those responsible, then Rod was to break with strict police procedures (something that Tony was used to doing - when he thought it necessary) and to inform Cheryl accordingly, not holding anything back.

After Rod, had told Cheryl that those at the Mambali police post had been killed, he went on to tell her that Tony, was now in hot pursuit of the killers.

Cheryl fully understood the possibilities of what Rod was telling her, tears came to her eyes, she had always had foreboding when it came to Tony going after insurgents that came into his area. She knew that he had, up to now, always managed to come through each contact, without so much as a scratch, but she also knew, how one of Tony's squad mates had been seriously injured in one sortie they had been on.

She knew that the Police Force, was Tony's life....his pride....and she knew she would never ever try and get him to give it up...but all the same, it did not stop her worrying.

She thanked Rod for the call, and slowly hung up the phone, reaching over for a photo of Tony that she kept by her bed, of him in his winter uniform - she always thought that he looked so much smarter in his winter uniform, than he did in his summer one, and lovingly gazed at it for a long time, before eventually holding it to her breasts, hugging and rocking it gently.

Cheryl recalled how honest Tony had always been with her, as to his past life. She cherished some of his tales, like how he and two of his mates,

Member In Charges of the Figtree and Matopos police stations, Roger and Dick, would always try and arrange to come in for their "Once a month shopping "trips into Bulawayo, together.

On one of these occasions Tony had told her, how after having had "quite a few beers," they went to the Fenella Redrup, Hostel for single women, and started to sing to them, whilst standing under a lamppost. When the "warden" had told them to clear off, and they had stayed, she said "I will call the police!" To which they all replied in unison "We ARE the police!"

Then there was the time when the three of them had gone to Bulawayo's finest hotel. Not having ties, they were kindly lent ties by the receptionist; otherwise they would not have been able to gain entrance. So they went to the "bar "had a drink, and then went upstairs to the dining room, and there they were ushered to a "table for three", amongst all the "gentry" in their finest "bib and tuckers".

They ordered the soup, which on its arrival the three of them, picking up their spoons in unison, took a sip, then throwing their chairs backwards, they fell to the floor, grasping their throats and gasping out loud as possible, so all could hear "It's the Soup...It's the SOUP!" This caused many of the others who were eating their soup at the time, to quickly drop their spoons in horror of being affected in the same way! The three of them were un-ceremoniously, taken from the Hotel, and after having handed back their "ties", were ordered out from the Hotel, and banned from returning!

Cheryl, chuckled to herself, and held the photo of Tony tighter to her, as she went on to recall how Tony had told her of another occasion when the "three," had again come in for their shopping, and after having quite a few beers together, were passing the Central Charge Office in Bulawayo, when Dick produced a "starting pistol" which he then dared Tony to fire in the Charge Office! Well...to dare Tony to do a prank - was to see him do it! So sure enough, Tony had taken the pistol, then ever so slowly opening the door to the Charge Office, observed, that behind the counter, were the night shift members, going about their respective duties, some standing, others sitting at their desks typing, so Tony thrust his hand holding the pistol in, and shouted "DIE...You Pigs!!" and with that fired the starting pistol....which had all those inside, diving for cover, as the three outside ran down the street, killing themselves with laughter. Their laughter though was not long lived, for it was only a little while, when, a Landrover pulled up in front of them, another behind, it was the "Riot Squad", who were on duty that week, and Tony, still had the starting pistol in his hand, so they surrounded them, weapons raised, ordered them to drop the gun, and without listening to the explanations that the three tried vainly to put across, bundled them roughly into the back of one of the Landrovers, and took them back to the main police station, where they were taken down to the lockup area. After a while they were all taken upstairs, to the Charge Office, where the duty Inspector, was waiting for them. As they came up the stairs, with Tony in the lead of the three, the Inspector suddenly recognized Tony, he said "OH...NO...not you Woody... oh and you two, the terrible trio!" and then taking them into his office, gave what appeared, to those watching through the windows from the Charge Office, a tongue lashing...but if the truth be known, the poor Inspector was trying so hard to control his laughter, wishing that he had been in on the prank himself, then told them "Go on - get out of here - go back to your stations, and next time when you come in, do so on my day off...won't you?"

"Oh...you were terrible, Tony" Cheryl said to herself - by the remembrance of these "tales" was taking her mind off the very serious situation that she knew, that Tony would now be facing.

Tony had always told her of his friendship with the African populace, and Tazwinga, and Chief Beyulah in particular, and how he had their respect in return. He told her how on one occasion, when he and Tazwinga were chasing a wanted murderer, how they had come to the chief's kraal, late in the evening, and the kindly old chief, had offered them his kraal, stating that they could sleep the night - which was most welcome, as they were tired from the chase- and so Tony was shown to the "guest hut", in which he was surprised to find a "double" bed, with clean, crisp sheets, and a blanket and pillows, all neatly laid out.

He told how, being so tired, he got out of his uniform, stripped naked, and wearily slipped in between the cool sheets, and was just about to turn out the Hurricane lamp, when there was a knock on the door. He said "Come in" expecting Tazwinga to come in, with some request - but instead in walked Beyulah's senior wife, and behind her, was her eldest daughter, a very attractive nubile maiden, her light brown skin, and gleaming white teeth were the things that he first noticed. She wore only a small thong, with a square piece of animal skin, at the front and rear, her top was bare, her pert ample breasts stood out, nipples erect, and as Tony looked on, the chief's wife then informed him, that Beyulah had sent her, to provide the daughter for Tony's comfort, for the night!

This indeed was a very high honor. One that the chief rarely made, to just anyone, and Tony felt a warm bond of closeness, that he knew existed between him and the chief, so to refuse this "offer" would have been a great insult! So he told the senior wife to thank the chief for his kindness, and how as she left closing the door, he wondered how he would work this problem out.

The chiefs daughter, walked over and locked the door, and then slowly approached the bed, as she got up to the opposite side to where Tony sat, with the sheet covering his nakedness, she undid the thong, and completely naked, she climbed onto the bed and slid under the sheet, smiling sweetly, her whiter than white perfect teeth, catching Tony's attention again, she realizing how highly her father must have thought of this "white policeman" to make such an offer, and that she, as an obedient daughter, would carry out her father's wishes, to the last degree, and she gave herself to him...more than once...during their night together!

Of course this did place Tony in a dilemma, for if such knowledge ever leaked out, then he would incur the wrath of many a superior officer, and would most certainly be put on the miscegenation file that the CID (Criminal Investigation Department) held of those who were known to have slept with women of another race (even though it was not perhaps done in the strict sense of inter breeding) be it either with an African or coloured (a half caste - whose one parent was African, the other European). In fact Tony had always told Cheryl how he really felt sorry for the coloured, as they were not trusted or liked by either the Africans - who thought there were spies for the "whites", and distrusted by the majority of whites, who regarded them as spies for the "Blacks!" So they were caught in "no man's land!"

In fact Tony had told her how when he was first stationed at Gwanda, he had come across such a sad case involving a coloured young man. His mother was an African Woman, who lived in the African Township, where "No coloured or white persons were allowed - except of course police and other officials whilst on duty." How this young lad would often go to visit his mother, only to be arrested by the "compound police" and brought to the BSA Police Charge Office - where Tony had seen him, and how the lad had broken down and cried and said that he only wanted to visit his mother! Which just highlighted the sorry situation - it was not his fault, after all!

If knowledge of Tony having been with the chief's daughter overnight, ever came out, irrespective of the fact that to have refused would have been an insult to the Chief, then he too would have been viewed with disgust by many serving members as a "Kaffir Lover," something that always made Tony smile when he heard people use this term, because it was known that many of the Afrikaans farmers, and other High Officials - in all walks of life, were often seen picking up the African Prostitutes! Talk about double standards.

Cheryl was so glad that Tony had never tried to cover up or lie about the number of different "sexual" partners he had had- most of whom were what could be referred to as just "one night stands" normally over the periods of his being in Bulawayo for his once a month shopping trips.

Cheryl recalled, one tale that Tony had related to her. After a night out on the "tiles" he had woken the next morning in bed with a stunning blonde, and crept out, to return to his station. Due to the heavy rains one of the rivers was overflowing, over the bridge, and he could not cross, so had to spend the night in the Landrover - waiting for the waters to recede sufficiently to allow him to be able to cross. He had with him, of course the shopping which included the "fresh" supplies of meat i.e. bacon, sausages etc. He was concerned that some of these might be going off by the time he got to the station - so on his arrival had his batman cook it straight away.

The next day, Tony woke with a rash all over his body, where ever his shorts and tunic covered! He immediately panicked - thinking the worst of that blonde he had been with! So he proceeded over to the Chelenyemba Mission and confided to Major Munn, who very discreetly had said "Well Tony, you do have to travel all over, and use many "out of the way" toilets out here in the bush "and then arranged for urine and blood samples to be sent off, to check, in case he had picked up a venereal disease!

A few days later the rash vanished, and Tony forgot all about the matter. A week later, he had been relaxing in the bath, when Rod knocked on the bathroom door and said "I have just come back from the Bidi Area, I called in to the Chelenyemba Mission on the way back - saw Major Munn, she said I was to tell you that your results have come back...they are positive...if that means anything to you?"

Tony told Cheryl, that he had nearly drowned! Positive...oh no...not the dreaded! Anyway he then got hold of his batman, told him that he had a nasty "chest" disease - but to not contaminate anyone else, had his batman to mark off, plate, cup, glass, spoon, knife fork etc, and to always give these to Tony, and wash them separately!

When Tony had eventually come out of the bath, Rod had given Tony tablets that Major Munn had given him, for Tony to take. Tony had religiously taken these every day!

A week later, he was sitting in his office, at Sun Yet Sen, when he saw dust from an approaching vehicle, coming from the Antelope mine area. As it got closer, he recognized it as the Mercedes, belonging to the local GMO (General Medical Officer) from the Antelope Hospital. She was a large German woman, in fact a titled Baroness!

"Oh, I hope she does not stop "Tony said to himself, as the car got nearer, then he heard the engine begin to slow and the car slowed down and eventually pulled into the police camp.

Out got the GMO and she came marching over. Seeing Tony was on his own, she walked into his office and sat down.

Tony greeted her, but pretended to be extremely busy, avoiding looking at her, avoiding any eye contact, as he knew that she as the GMO would also know of his test results and he certainly did not want to face her! When all the conversation "dried up," the GMO said "Oh...by the way...your results came back"

Tony nearly choked...he had to look at her now, as he did so he said "Yes...I...er...I know" he muttered, and the GMO looked at him and said "How could you know, I only got them today?" And as I had guessed - it must have been something that you ate...because all the tests proved negative." Tony could not believe his ears...he explained to the GMO what Major Munn had said, showing the GMO the tablets that he had been taking, which the GMO looked at, and then burst out laughing! When she eventually calmed down, she explained that the tablets were in fact "sugar tablets." Major Munn, known for her sense of humor - had played the ultimate joke on Tony, with the help of Rod.

Rod would not forget the matter either, for as a result, he had been called into Tony's Office after the GMO had left, and was given a two week, walking patrol along the Shashe River- mapping every possible crossing point he could find!

"Oh Tony "Cheryl laughed to herself - these memories had made her forget for a moment the danger he could be in, and had alleviated the sadness she had earlier felt.

She lifted the photo of Tony up, looking at it tenderly, and silently prayed that Tony would come through this present contact, safe once again.

20

Bison slowly crawled from behind the sofa, and edged his way to the door, which he now closed and locked. "Well done Toby, you did real good, old friend" he said, and Toby grinned, his white teeth showing up in the dark "You taught your servant well, Nkosi - but they will come again - can we keep them at bay - we do not even know how many of them there are" and Bison knew this to be true, he had no idea how big this gang was, and he could not really answer his trusty servant's question, as he really did not know if they would be able to continue to hold them off" But we will damn well try " he thought to himself.

He turned to Toby and said "We will move into the bedroom, we can see the water tower better from there, seeing both sides, and wait for them to show themselves, and see what we can do." He and Toby then carefully eased their way down the corridor, passed the body of the dead terrorist, as they did so, Bison bent down and picked up the AK rifle from the dead man's right hand, prising it free from the death grip "That will give me a few extra rounds "he said to himself as he and Toby continued on into the bedroom.

Ngonga had seen the door of the living room close. He waited for a few seconds, and then reached for one of his grenades. "So you want to hole up in there eh...well Ndlovu, closing that door will not protect you...I have a nice little present for you "as he said this, he stood up, pulled the pin from the grenade, and, aiming at the bay window, threw with all his might.

His aim was true - the grenade broke through the glass window, and rolled through the living room, into the dining room area, coming to rest under the dining room table, where Toby's wife and son huddled together.

The grenade came to rest, just a few inches from them. They both looked at it, and at each other, and then back at the grenade again. They had no idea, what this contraption, that had been thrown into the building was, and perhaps fortunately, they did not have time to think what it may be, for as they looked at it, and the son, stretched his hand out to pick the item up, it exploded, killing them both instantly, demolishing the dining room furniture, and leaving a crater in the floor. The shockwave of the explosion sent Toby falling onto Bison, and they both collapsed onto the floor, their ears still ringing from the sound of the explosion, not realizing at this stage, that Toby's wife and son had been killed in that explosion.

They got up and eased their way to the window, which Bison now slowly opened, so that they had a clear view, and they lay side by side, with their weapons trained on the water tower, Bison to the right side, and Toby, who had now been handed the AK47 rifle, to the left side." Wait till you have a good view before you fire "Bison told Toby "we don't want to give away our position, unless we are sure we can get a killing shot" he continued. They waited together, Bison forgetting about the pain and bleeding from his shoulder, like a wounded buffalo, he was now at his most dangerous.

*****

Goliath had led Tony, Tazwinga and the chasing group up to the old brick garage that Bison had since turned into a stable for his horse, when the explosion of the hand grenade inside the ranch house rocked them all, and they crouched down low. "Bloody hell" Tony exclaimed "The bastards are really out to get old Bison" he said, not realizing that Ngonga was under the impression that it was Tony in the house.

Goliath as the norm in these situations, once leading them up to the enemy, withdrew, letting the entire police chasing group through, so that he now brought up the rear, but as always, even from this position he did not miss a thing that was happening.

From where they were, they could see in the moonlight the steel windmill in front of them, and the water tower, which was over to the left, and over to the right was the main house. Tony motioned to Tazwinga, who sidled up to him "Send six round to the back of the house - you, I and the other four will go over to the windmill" he said. Tazwinga chose six, gave them their orders, and they watched, rifles at the ready, as these six slid out from behind the stable, and approached the kitchen area of the house.

Once they had disappeared, Tony Tazwinga and the other four Constables, with Goliath in tow, moved slowly towards the steel windmill.

Toby, was straining his old tired eyes to see the water tower, unaware at this stage that his wife and son lay killed, by the grenade, when he suddenly caught sight of movement from the left side of the water tower. He rubbed his tired old eyes, blinking, and peered out again...Yes...there it was...the figure of a man, very slowly edging his way round the water tower, his back pressed up against the tower, his AK 47 rifle held in his arms, at an angle across his chest. Toby aimed at the darkened figure and squeezed the trigger, four to six rounds, went off kicking up spurts of dust by the feet of the terrorist, who quickly withdrew back behind the water tower once again.

Toby was not used to this type of weapon, and his aim was not true, he felt that he had let his master down and sighing, turned and said "sorry...Nkosi...I missed." "That's all right, old friend "Bison replied "can't get one every time...but watch out now, because they know where we are - another grenade could come our way, let's go back to the living room again "and they both shuffled out of the bedroom, down the corridor once more, over the dead terrorists, and back into the living room area, which had partly been wrecked in the explosion.

It was only then, that Toby suddenly saw the remains of his wife and son, parts of which had been scattered in the explosion all over the room, and he gave out a low cry of anguish.

Bison seeing what had happened, was moved to tears for his faithful old servant, went over and placed his arm consolingly on Toby's shoulder stating "Sorry, my friend, I'm really so sorry - we will take as many of them down as we can for this, this I promise you," and Toby reached up, squeezed Bison's hand, and they took up their positions by the bay window, through which the grenade had been thrown.

Tony, Tazwinga, Goliath and the four Constables had just arrived at the windmill when the shots were fired from the house. They saw that the shots were aimed at the water tower, and Tony counted himself to be lucky, that now at least they knew where the terrorists were grouped.

Ngonga too, heard the shots, and immediately realized that they were from the AK 47 rifle, with which his gang were armed, and knew that it must have been taken from the dead terrorist in the house...suddenly it dawned on him...he had been mistaken...Ndlovu was not in the house! He had miscalculated...it was those two old men, Toby and Mr. Pritzkow - "The old white buzzard...I did not get a clean strike...he is alive...we have wasted much time and ammunition here now, as well as losing men "and once again he gave a shudder, as he realized too, that Ndlovu, and the chasing group would have heard all the shooting and explosion, and it would not be long before they would be here.

Ngonga now started to formulate a plan to leave the ranch. The thought of his being here when Ndlovu arrived, was now becoming a worry to him, and he slowly began to realise that he would not be able to now, not with only two other members left, have any hope at all at beating that chasing group. "I should have ambushed them before they got here...or should have backtracked and attacked them whilst they were asleep "he said to himself, realizing now the mistakes that he had made. The thought of his being killed made him shiver...no...Not him...not Ngonga.

The thought of capture filled him with dread...captured...by Ndlovu, and the chasing group, all of whom would personally know him...he could not face that...especially after what he had done to their comrades at the Mambali post.

Ngonga called the two remaining gang members together "Right" he said in his authoritative voice "I am going to circle, wide out, and approach the house from the rear, and surprise them - they will not expect anyone to do that - whilst you two keep firing at them from here, to make them still think that we are all still here at this spot, and don't forget the grenades, if you get a chance to use them, I will give you a yell once I have disposed of those in the house" he continued cockily.

The two thought to themselves, what a brave leader they had, to try and accomplish that on his own, and so sure of himself, made them think that he would not fail either, not knowing that in reality, that was the furthermost thought in Ngonga's head, he had already planned to sneak away, and to leave these two to their fate!

Ngonga slipped away quietly, leaving his two gang members, and started to head out towards the Champion Ranch, from there he would be able to follow the Shashani River, down to where it joined the Shashe River, and then come back up the Shashe River till he found a crossing point, back to the safety of Botswana.

He would get together a larger group for the next time. "And then...Ndlovu, I will return for you...you have not won...that dream will not come true this time" he gave out a nervous laugh, as he pushed through the thorn bushes and continued heading away from the ranch house as quickly as he could, he wanted to put as much space between him and his comrades, so that when the end came, which he knew would come, he would have a good head start on Ndlovu.

The two remaining members, loyal to their leader, and believing all that he said, slowly circled the water tower, one to each side, and once having the ranch house in view opened fire at the same time, pouring bullets into the living room, and bedroom areas, smashing the bay window and the bedroom window to pieces, glass flew in all directions as the bullets thudded into furniture and walls and ricocheted about. The noise in the still night air was deafening.

The six constables had by then entered the house, by the kitchen door, and had called out to Bison and Toby who they were, as they came down the corridor, stepping over the dead terrorist, they were glad they had done so, not wanting to end up like him! They then took up positions with Toby and Bison.

As the fusillade of shots rained through the bay windows glass, slivers of glass pierced one of the constables eyes, he yelled out in pain, falling back into the arms of one of his fellow members, screaming in pain, as blood flowed from both eyes!

Tony, Tazwinga and the other four constables, were at the windmill when the two terrorists opened fire. From where they stood, they could make out the figure of the one terrorist, up against the side of the water tower. After he had fired into the house, he had crouched low, and was in fact heading towards the windmill, where they were, crouching low to avoid detection from the ranch house, not knowing that he was heading straight towards them, and his death,

Tony raised his FN Rifle, aiming at the ghostly figure, and fired. Six bullets shot out of the rifle, and struck the terrorist, just below the line of his chin and ploughed into his ribcage. The force of the bullets pushed the terrorist backwards, his feet came over in a form of a backward somersault, and his death cries tore through the night.

The remaining terrorist, seeing his comrade fall back against the water tower, raised his AK47 rifle, and noting from where the shots had come, trained his weapon onto the windmill, and sent a hail of bullets towards it.

From what little cover there was at the windmill, one of the four constables was struck in the head by one bullet, his body was thrown back onto a nearby knobthorn bush, where he died, and hung there like a scarecrow. One or two of the other bullets struck the steel windmill, and the bullets shattered, sending particles of the bullet whizzing off in all directions. A piece of this struck Tony in his forearm, about six inches from his wrist. Tony felt a burning sensation, and then the warm flow of blood. He automatically dropped his weapon, reaching down with his right hand over to grab his left arm, just below the elbow, tried to stem the flow of blood. "Damn it Taz "he said "I've been hit," and he turned to look at Tazwinga, and for a moment his blood ran cold, for Tazwinga's head was a mass of blood, bleeding from numerous pieces of shattered bullets, that had struck his head, the blood running freely down his face and neck, down onto his uniform. Tony bent down towards his dear friend, and gave a sigh of relief when Tazwinga said "me, too...sir...and in many places it seems".

As the others returned fire, Tony and Tazwinga crawled back to the old garage, which was now a stable. Once there Goliath went and fetched some water, and returning used this to wash both Tazwinga's head, and Tony's arm, and they were then able to see the extent of the wound.

A fragment of the bullet still protruded from Tony's arm, and Tony noticed that it had imbedded itself so very close to the main artery - but thankfully had missed it. Tazwinga on the other hand had five separate pieces imbedded in his head, and of course a cut of any kind on the head was always known for its bleeding, but again thankfully, none of these were causing any permanent damage, and they both sank down onto their haunches, smiling at each other. "Boss" Tazwinga said "That was close" "That's for sure" Tony replied "Nearly ended our drinking and womanizing days, eh?" and they both gave a chuckle. Bandages were applied, and they then both gave attention to the job, still at hand.

Goliath, ever diligent, came up to Tony and Tazwinga and said that he had seen the figure of Ngonga slink off, leaving his two comrades. "Taz" Tony said "will you remain here and get that last one, whilst I go with Goliath after Ngonga...? I don't want him getting away...not again."

"Go" Tazwinga replied" I know that he won't get away from you - Goliath will ensure that ...go don't worry...we will mop up here "and he clasped Tony's hand tightly "Go with the wind, and accomplish what has to be done...Ndlovu" he said, and with that Tony picked up his FN rifle and followed Goliath, as they skirted the water tower, and it was not long before Goliath had picked up Ngonga's spoor. "He is heading off towards Champion Ranch...that's a long route to get to the Shashe river, and there is no safe crossing point there, the nearest is the one due south of this ranch- we will go straight...to the nearest crossing point...he will have to come there...Ndlovu, and we will be waiting for him" and he turned and grinned at Tony.

Tony was loathe to give up the actual chase, but trusted this little bushman, when it came to matters of bush lore, and knew that if Goliath said, that there was only one safe crossing point, and that Ngonga would have to come to it, then so be it, that's where they would go, and wait for him.

As Goliath grinned Tony could not help but notice those white teeth again, something that always amazed Tony was how nearly all the Africans, in the homelands particularly, seemed to always have such great looking, whiter than white teeth, yet the majority of them never ever used a toothbrush or toothpaste, preferring instead, to use the gnawed end of a twig! "Must be something in it, or in their diet" Tony mused to himself, as he clasped Goliath's shoulder, and said "Let's go then - don't want to be late do we?" Goliath knew how much it meant to Tony to catch up and arrest, rather than kill Ngonga, but knowing too that if push came to shove, that Tony would not hesitate to kill Ngonga.

The last remaining terrorist, decided to use his grenade to kill as many as he could, and drawing one out, he pulled the pin, and threw it at the windmill, where he presumed the chasing group were still gathered. The grenade landed at the foot of one of the steel "legs" of the windmill, where it exploded throwing up large chunks of earth, weakening the windmills legs, leaving a large crater, and the windmill, as if in slow motion, with a loud creaking noise, slowly toppled over.

The terrorist then turned towards the house, firing rapidly, spraying the whole house with bullets, and then pulled out another grenade, which he intended to lob once again, through the bay window of the house, in doing so would have caused quite a few deaths of those therein.

He pulled the pin, holding the grenade in his hand, ready to throw, when a sudden burst of FN fire, from Tazwinga, who had seen what his intentions were, caught him in the wrist, severing the right wrist just about right off, it hung in threads, and the grenade fell at his feet. The terrorist screamed in agony, as blood pulsated from the end of his tattered arm, forgetting for a moment about the grenade, and when he remembered it, with a look of horror, he started to move, but before he could do so, the grenade exploded! The already dead terrorist that was lying next to the grenade was hurtled upwards, the head having taken most of the blast, was severed from the main body. The terrorist that had intended to throw the grenade, was thrown into the air, both his feet having been blown off in the blast, and was hurtled into the bushes, screaming in agony, looking at his lower body where his legs should have been, seeing that there was nothing there, and he died, and a deathly, eerie calm and quiet befell the area.

Tazwinga called to each of the chasing group in turn, who answered him, and then called to the house where Bison answered, and they all got up and met on the grassy green lawn, by the verandah, where hours earlier Bison had been taking in a breath of fresh air, admiring, the quiet, and peaceful night!

Tazwinga got onto the radio, called Sun Yet Sen and made his report. Rod took the call and immediately contacted the Officer Commanding at Gwanda, Gus Armstrong and relayed the news to him.

Gus Armstrong, phoned down to the police mess, and had the helicopter pilot meet him at the heliport, and within a few minutes they were airborne, heading for the Nazeby Ranch South, where they used the helicopter to ferry those wounded to hospital in Gwanda, where they could get full medical attention, as soon as they arrived. Gus had already contacted the hospital at Gwanda, and they had their doctors and staff, on stand-by awaiting, the wounded.

21

Ngonga was still running blindly through the bushes, towards Champion Ranch, and the Shashani River. He heard the continued gunfire, and the sound of the two grenade explosions, and had a feeling of pride, at the loyalty of those two remaining gang members that he had left behind, knowing that they were giving their all, which was buying him more time to make good his escape.

He had not gone much further, when he pulled up sharply. He stopped; listened...straining his ears...all that could be heard was the night noises. He waited for several minutes, hearing nothing...no more gunfire...no more grenade explosions....nothing...and slowly it dawned on him...it was all over....those two had given their all...

He knew that Ndlovu would soon find out that he was not amongst the casualties, and once again the chase would be on, with that little bushman leading it "Damn you...Ndlovu...will you not give up?" he cursed, He and started to run wildly through the bushes once again, the thorn bushes tearing at his uniform and skin as he did so, pushing on desperately...he just had to get to the safety of Botswana. He paused for breath by a large Baobab tree, firstly to relieve himself, and then sat down to have a drink of water, for his mouth was parched.

Whilst sitting there, he began to think of just what he would say when he got back to the terrorist camps, as to what had happened - and how those with him had died.

Of course he would say that they all died gloriously...in the line of freedom, that much he did know...but what he wanted...was to glorify the account, so that his survival would appear even more spectacular.

YES...he would concoct a glorified account of bravery and heroism that was for sure - just thinking about it actually made him start to believe, that was what had happened, and that he was really now a conquering hero! His head spinning in self adoration, and the thought of the fine reception he would get at the various camps. All of this made him forget his actual situation, and he rose, and with head held high, walked down to the

Shashani river, with a gleeful jump of excitement, he now started to follow this river down to where it would join the Shashe river, and from there, he would locate the first crossing place, and there, back to Botswana...and the best news...was that there had not even been the slightest movement seen, or noise detected, of the chasing group, so confident was he that he had managed to give them the slip, or that they were so far behind, that they could not catch him...OR...had his two gang members, actually managed to wound, or even kill, Ndlovu...Oh yes...maybe that's why there was no chasing group. He actually believed this too, and so his pace lessened, there was now no need for any rush at all, and he slung his rifle, over his shoulder, no need to carry it ready to fight anymore ...so he thought!

Tony and Goliath had continued at a quickened pace, weaving in and out of the bushes, no longer being slowed by Goliath having to follow a spoor, as they were not going to follow Ngonga on his long route, but just head straight to the Shashe River, and the crossing point.

They too heard the gunfire, the sound of a fierce firefight, and then the sound of two grenade explosions - Tony was concerned for those they had left behind, especially with the grenade explosions- knowing the devastation they could cause.

As they headed on, the two of them, too, suddenly paused...there was no more gunfire, no more explosions, and Tony realized, that they had won the battle...now there was only one outstanding piece of business that had to be taken care of, and he and Goliath, after an exchange of smiling glances and a firm handshake on the "victory", continued on in their quest to capture Ngonga.

22

The journey by helicopter took just under an hour, and they arrived overhead of the Nazeby South Ranch, as the sun broke through. Flying over the ranch house, they could clearly see the damage. The Windmill was down onto its side, the crater from the explosion clearly seen, as was the crater by the water tower, the tower having miraculously withstood the blast. As they hovered lower, they could see the pock marks of bullets on the water tower, all over the house, they noticed too, the roof of the house in one section, having been blown off "Oh Hell" Gus said to himself "A grenade was thrown in there - hope many were not killed."

The pilot gently settled the helicopter down on the front lawn, where all those still standing were gathered. The helicopter was still a few yards from the ground, when Gus Armstrong jumped out, and crouching low to avoid the Rota blades, ran over to where Tazwinga and Bison, and the others stood. Tazwinga the ever diligent policeman called the chasing group to attention, and coming to attention himself, snapped out a salute to his bloodied head, which was immediately returned by Gus who said "Stand the men at ease, please Tazwinga, they deserve to be after what they have been through" then after a brief pause asked "Are you O.K. Sergeant Major?" as he noticed the bloodstained bandage and uniform and dried blood down the sides of Tazwinga's face "Yes Sir... no permanent damage, just fragments of a bullet or bullets in my scalp" but then continued "But we have lost one member in death, and have another with serious eye injuries" and as he paused Gus intervened saying "Get yourself and the one with the eye injury over to the helicopter- it will take you to the Gwanda Hospital for treatment," and then turned and headed over to where Bison stood.

"Hello, Bison" he said, and shook Bison's, one good hand "I see you need some looking at too, so if you would like to get yourself over to the helicopter, it will take you to the Hospital, and bring you back once you have been properly patched up. O.K.?" he asked.

Bison replied "Yeah- fine thanks Gus...Toby's wife and son were killed by the grenade blast in the house" he paused in grief. For a moment, then continued "Tony and Goliath have gone after the leader...it's that damned ex constable Ngonga...I hope they catch the bastard!"

Gus replied "Sorry to hear of the deaths...all round...since this sorry show started...nasty business...yeah I heard it was ex PC Ngonga at the head of this...would you credit it...yes I heard that Tony and Goliath have continued after them...so I'm with you...hope they get the swine! You don't mind if I set up camp here, till we hear the outcome?" He asked. "Not at all" Bison replied, as he headed over towards the waiting helicopter. He came up to Toby, the two warmly embraced, both openly, unashamedly crying with grief over the deaths of Toby's wife and son, and then separating, Bison sauntered over and got into the helicopter, which slowly started to rise, showering dust and grass particles over all those nearby, as is took off and headed back towards Gwanda.

As the helicopter took off, two Landrovers pulled up. Rod was in the lead one. He got out, and crossed over to where his Officer Commanding stood, saluted and said "We have come to collect the dead, ours and theirs, and render any other assistance we can sir" he concluded.

"Fine" Gus replied, and he walked into the house surveying the damage, and noticed that Toby had lovingly collected the remains of his wife and son, and placed these in two blankets. Outside the dead terrorists had been laid out, with identification tags attached to their ankles, their arms and ammunition were all gathered, as were the shotguns that they had taken from the Mambali police post. The bodies had then been placed in body bags, and put into the second Landrover to be transported back to the Sun Yet Sen police station.

The remaining chasing group, then made a request, and were given permission to stay at Nazeby South, till the outcome of the final episode would be known, this was only fitting under the circumstances.

Gus then got onto the phone, which miraculously was still working, it was a party-line, and with three long rings, and two short rings, got through to Mrs. Day - who had been blissfully unaware of what had been happening down at the Nazeby South Ranch, and told her all that had occurred, reassuring her that Bison seemed O.K. and had gone to have his wound properly treated at the Gwanda Hospital.

Gus knowing Tony so well, and how procedures, were there for him to overlook at times, turned to Rod and said "Have you kept Cheryl informed of developments" he paused, and could see the unease on Rod's face...he was unsure just what to say...to say yes would mean an admittance of Tony's breaking of police procedure...but Gus knew by this that it had been done, as he had expected, so putting the lad out of his misery said "If not...then I would jolly well hurry up and do so...otherwise you could well feel my boot, up your rear! Let her know that he has been slightly wounded...nothing serious, and that he has gone after the leader, and that we will contact her again, as soon as we know more ourselves. Rod's face showed signs of massive relief, "Yes, sir" he said, as he too then reached for the telephone, and giving the handle a long hard twirl, got through to the telephone operator at Antelope, and asked to be put through to Cheryl's number in Bulawayo.

Cheryl was having breakfast at the time that the call came through. She reached up and picked up the phone, and hearing it was Rod on the other end, her face went white, and she started to tremble.

Rod quickly explained what the situation was and she asked "And Tony?" Rod went on to explain that he had been injured...on hearing her gasp at the other end, hurried on to say, that it was not serious, and that he and Goliath had gone after the ring leader, and tried hard to reassure her that all would be O.K. and that she was not to worry, adding that he would keep her informed, as soon as they had more details ending saying that his Officer Commanding Gus Armstrong had said if he did not keep her informed he would be in trouble!

But for Cheryl, being so far from all the action, and not being able to talk to Tony herself, she still had reservations. She would only really and truly be able to relax, once she was able to talk to Tony himself.

She thanked Rod, nonetheless, for his call, but sitting there all alone her mind was going through the worst scenarios, these bringing tears to her eyes, which ran down her cheeks, and fell in droplets, splashing down onto the breakfast table, as she contemplated Tony being killed, his burial, and life without the one she so dearly loved, the one she wanted to live with and share the rest of her life with.

She got herself into such a state, before sanity prevailed, and she calmed down, and recalled once again all the previous sorties that Tony had been on, and had come through, without so much as a scratch...and she started to assure herself, that this time would be no different "He will be O.K...he will be O.K." she kept repeating to herself, as she sat, hugging her knees, looking at the photo of Tony. She then made a phone call to her manageress, explaining briefly the situation, and asked to take the rest of the day off, so she could be at hand, to receive whatever news was to come her way that day.

23

Goliath led Tony through to an opening from the forest, where they joined a path. "This is the only safe crossing place this far down "Goliath said "Ngonga will have to double back from where the Shashani river joins the Shashe, and he will have to come back to here...come...we will wait for him, down on the river's edge "and they slowly walked down the embankment, and down to the river's edge, where there was a thicket of tangled Borassus Palm trees and bushes, interleaved with the long brown grass, brown from the drought, at the top, greener as it got nearer the earth, being watered by the Shashe river.

It was a perfect "hide-out," as they could observe the pathway, leading up and down the bank from the trees.

They settled down to wait, the bandage over the shrapnel in Tony's arm still bloodstained, and the arm, at the site of entry was throbbing, but Tony put this aside, as he kept his eyes firmly fixed on the pathway, waiting for Ngonga to appear- thus was the faith that he had in Goliath's assurance that there was no other crossing point further downstream.

As they settled down, a movement caught Tony's eyes, and he peered hard and long, till out of the grass came a flock of Guinea Fowl, their bluish grey feathers now clearly seen, as they pecked at whatever they could find to eat, and slowly as a flock, moved till they were once more out of sight. On the far bank he caught sight of a Hammerkop, a brown medium sized wading bird, so called because of a peculiar crest, giving the head a distinctive hammer shaped profile. He watched this too, till it passed out of sight, all this relaxing him, so that he settled down, his breathing evened, after their journey down to this spot.

*****

Ngonga came out from the undergrowth at the point where the Shashani and Shashe rivers met, and then realized that in his haste, and perhaps not giving enough thought to where he was going, but rather to what he was going to do, once back safely in Zambia, had come out, too far down, from the known safe crossing point.

He cursed then added "No matter... only about a mile or so upstream, still no sign of anyone following...soon be in safety," and he rejoined the pathway that ran alongside the Shashe river, and started on his way up stream.

The first alert that Tony and Goliath had was when the cry from a Gray Loire bird perched atop of one of the trees gave its sudden "GO WAY" call, which echoed over the stillness.

Tony and Goliath crouched even lower, peering up along the path. A touch on Tony's shoulder by Goliath, and his scrawny hand pointed up ahead.

Tony looked and looked, straining his eyes, and then

suddenly he saw it...it was the top of a head, bobbing up and down, above the level of the bushes, as the person unhurriedly strode along.

Tony slid the safety catch off his rifle, and waited...could this be Ngonga? He could hear his heartbeat in his ears, his adrenaline was flowing, his excitement mounting, "Calm down" he told himself.

A few moments longer and there...round the corner, out of the bushes, striding along the path, like a person on a Sunday afternoon stroll, came Ngonga. His AK 47 rifle was slung across his back; obviously he was so sure of himself that he was not even contemplating that anyone could possibly be ahead of him. No one that could do him any harm, anyway, and from his manner, it appeared that he was in fact sure that he had eluded his chasers, and was now home and free!

Ngonga came down the embankment, onto the river sand, and slowly started to walk towards the river's edge, and that's when Tony called out "Ngonga- STOP"

Ngonga froze for an instant, recognizing Ndlovu's voice. His head spun "NO...it could not be... his ears were playing tricks." then Tony's voice brought him back to reality "DON'T MOVE! It's all over. Move and I will shoot and drop you where you stand" and he could hear the venom in Tony's voice.

Ngonga stood motionless for a moment, then reacted. He reached for his AK rifle, Tony saw the move...and not wanting to kill Ngonga, Tony aimed and shot, the bullet struck Ngonga on his right thigh, only a flesh wound - no broken bones or serious injury, but enough to surprise Ngonga, who recoiled, slipped and fell, dropping his rifle as he did so.

Ngonga recovered, and scrambled to his feet, and started to run, at a limp down the riverbed. Tony passed his rifle over to Goliath and with agility seldom seen of someone his portly shape, sprang out of the bushes, and gave chase.

Running in river sand, was at best a hard thing to do, but when you are carrying a flesh wound to your thigh as well, made it even harder to do, and Tony was rapidly closing the distance between the two of them.

Tony realized that his stamina would not last much longer. His mouth was already dry, his breathing rasping, so with one final effort, he launched himself into a jump at Ngonga.

Goliath, who was trotting behind, could not believe what he was seeing in his friend, as he took off, like a rocket, and came down, with all his two hundred and thirty pounds, on his knees, landing on Ngonga's midriff, knocking him down, and knocking the breath out of Ngonga.

It felt for a moment, to Ngonga, that indeed an elephant had knelt down upon him, and immediately his nightmare came back to haunt him "NDLOVU" he hissed through clenched teeth.

Ngonga's hand went down, and he pulled out his hunting knife from its sheath. Goliath who had been watching, yelled a warning to Tony, who thanks to his friends warning, was able to grab Ngonga's arm before he could bring the knife to bear, and they both struggled, rolling over and over, with Ngonga trying to force the knife into Tony's stomach - or anywhere would do, with Tony holding on trying to keep the knife away from his body.

They both got to their knees, and then managed to stand up on their feet, still locked in this stalemate, before Ngonga, with his wounded thigh, gave way, and he fell back against the rivers embankment.

As his back hit the bank, the pain from his leg made him wince, and he gave a little...and that was all that Tony was waiting for...he twisted the hand that held that wicked hunting knife, and put his weight behind it.

Ngonga's arm gave way, and folded in, bringing the knife down. The movement brought the knife down and across, with the sharp blade slicing through Ngonga's uniform, and it tore into his skin, cutting across his stomach up towards his ribs....and for now, this was just like his dream...first to be trampled on, and then he was impaled on the tusk...and here now was Ndlovu, having first landed with all his weight upon him, like the trampling of an elephant, and now this cutting open of his stomach, as if impaled on a tusk..." AAAGH...Ndlovu! You are the White Elephant, I saw in my dreams" he hissed as he collapsed, and Goliath who had been standing watching the proceedings, was over like a flash, and turning Ngonga over, grabbed his arms, and bound them behind his back, as Tony sank down to his knees and then sat down on the rivers bank, completely out of breath, but boy oh boy, ever so relieved that he had finally managed to "get his man!"

Goliath handed Tony his FN rifle, and then went and picked up Ngonga's AK47 rifle, and his hunting knife, and came back up to where Tony and Ngonga were. Tony was lying stretched out, on the river bank, taking in deep breaths of the clean air, as he looked up at the white cotton wool shaped clouds, drifting by in the blue sky, he had a quiet smile on his face, he was content, content at firstly at last getting this ex Constable Ngonga, still wanted for the murder he committed soon after his retirement-so at least now he would stand trial for that - but content also, for having been able to kill all those responsible for the outrage at Mambali, and to be able to bring back to stand trial, for that crime the ring leader, although not easing the pain of the deaths of those members, but some consolation nonetheless, but most of all content in the knowledge that he had come through, this contact, fortunately once again, without any serious injury, and so would be able to see Cheryl again, and he wondered how she would be coping with the knowledge that he was out here.

Goliath, came up and likewise lay down by his friend, a big smile on his face, as he reached over and placed his hand on Tony's shoulder "Aaah, Ndlovu - you have done it - you lived up to your name - may this also be told all round the area, so that all will see the folly of crossing you", Tony sat up and grasped the wiry bushman's hand, in a firm grip saying " Goliath-you know, that we would not even be here, if it was not for you- as so many times past, I am deeply in your debt, and will never forget the big part you played in this, which too must be told and retold - as people remember this day."

They sat having a refreshing drink from their canteens, and Ngonga, who was still lying face down, on the bank, his hands securely bound behind his back, groaned and said "When you two have quite finished talking and lying down, will you think about me? I am wounded, bleeding, and need urgent Medical attention, that is only my right as a prisoner of war! The Geneva Convention says it's so." Tony and Goliath exchanged glances, Tony said "Goliath, were my ears deceiving me or did that pile of dung speak?" Goliath looked over at Ngonga and back to Tony and said" No – Ndlovu - you must have been mistaken, for I have never ever heard of any dung being able to speak!" and they both chuckled, as they walked over to where Ngonga lay, and roughly, grabbing him, hurled him to his feet, amid cries of pain from him which they completely ignored.

Once up, they set off on their journey back towards Nazeby South Ranch, half walking half dragging Ngonga between them, his cries for a rest fell on deaf ears, as the death of those police members and the mutilation of the old man whose lip was cut off was still fresh in their memory.

To say that he was not "endeared" to them would be an understatement, and if the truth be told, many a thorn bush seemed to have somehow got between Tony and Goliath, and right into the dragged Ngonga!

After some time, they came into view of those at the ranch, who were silently waiting to hear from them, a cry of joy rang out as the first Constable in the chasing group recognized them, and this was followed by wild whoops of sheer delight, as each person saw, that there was Ngonga, being dragged between Tony and Goliath.

These whoops of delight brought Gus and Rod, running from the house, together with Bison, Tazwinga and Toby too.

The helicopter had since returned. Bison had had his shoulder seen to and had been released, being the hardy old man that he was, it was not as serious a wound, to his way of thinking, compared to what he had received, when being mauled by a leopard!

Tazwinga had had four of the five pieces of shrapnel removed from his scalp, one was too far imbedded, the Hospital had said that it would cause no trouble, and in fact could well work itself loose in due course. "Told you, you had a rock for a head, Taz "Tony teased him on hearing about this.

Gus came out and took Tony to one side, as Rod placed Ngonga under guard in the helicopter, and it took off once more for Gwanda, to deliver the prisoner, and then to return once more. As it rose up Gus said "Well done Woody! Great outcome - sorry about the deaths, but at least we not only have the bodies of those that did it, but also that Ngonga - still can't believe how someone with his vast police experience, could have turned so bad, so soon after retirement - just does not figure. Still, I do think, that before you do anything else, you had better make a phone call to someone...she has been waiting all day...must be getting quite worked up by now...so go ahead...then we will talk."

Tony walked over to the wrecked homestead, picked up the phone and got the telephone operator to put him through once more to Cheryl's number in Bulawayo.

The phone rang, and rang, and rang...Cheryl's heart missed a beat, and she stared at the phone, she was loathe to pick it up, scared of what she might hear, but eventually, slowly, picked up and hesitatingly said "H-e-l-l-o." Tony on the other end said "Hi, honey...it's me...Ndlovu....the White Elephant!" he paused, and what appeared to be an eternity passed before the realisation of what he had said, got through to Cheryl, she shrieked with delight, as her anxious waiting came to an end, and then realized that she was crying... tears of JOY. She asked Tony to tell her honestly how he was, and he related the events, his injury, and his finally getting Ngonga, and bringing him back....alive...to face up to what the courts would give him, for not only the murder of the woman at his home area, but the killing of all those at Mambali, and of Toby's dear wife and child. Having convinced Cheryl, he hung up the phone, and walked out and over to where Toby stood, head bent low in silent mourning for his wife and child. Tony slowly approached him, laid a hand on his shoulder, Toby turned, and seeing Tony, fell into Tony's arms, and together they stood, supporting one another, both openly crying for the deaths that had occurred, but both with some relief in the deaths of those responsible, and for the capture of Ngonga till Bison came to them together with Gus Armstrong, and Bison recalled the gallant effort old Toby had given him to overcome those who were attacking them, and all agreed that Toby should receive some worthy recognition for all he had done.

*****

Tony sat in his chair, watching the sun's rays falling on the mine, having finished the coffee Cheryl had brought to him earlier. She massaged his neck and shoulders, and then went into the bedroom. After about a quarter of an hour Cheryl came out of the bedroom and from behind him, she put her arms around him, "Oh darling, she said, how I wish those nightmares would leave you...but, I do have something to tell you "and as he turned

113

and lovingly looked at her, she continued "It was confirmed yesterday at the doctors, I'm pregnant!"

Tony took her in his arms, held her close, he too with tears of joy at the thought of the impending "parenthood" he looked at her and said "Just as well, for its time for this old bull elephant to retire ... and now with this coming event... it will be a boy... you know" Cheryl just looked at him, and said "Oh yes, you can guarantee that can you?" and Tony replied "Well...it has to be...yeah, a young, new elephant, ...the son...and heir... of NDLOVU - THE WHITE ELEPHANT!"

PART TWO

24

Bison Pritzkow slowly walked into his main farm house, having carried out his usual procedure - after dinner to stand on the verandah, watching the sun set. The sky was aglow, with a fiery red, as the sun slowly began to set. This day was no different from the thousands that he had done before.

He had settled on this ranch in the early 1950s. He had built this ranch up over the years, both Nazeby, and the Nazeby South, and then had purchased the adjoining ranch, Champion Ranch too. For the past 50 years he had continued running these - now well into his eighties, he still was that squat solid figure, he had always been. Burnt brown from the sun, his craggy face with many a wrinkle still had a ready smile for the simpler things, the things of nature, and this beauty of Africa. He loved the sunset, the animals, both wild and domestic that ran on these ranches, accepting the challenge of protecting his cattle from predators, but he had a hatred for those who would try to steal, or maim the animals by means of snares - the wire snares used trapped the animals as the steel lasso caught either round the neck or legs of the unfortunate beast, and the more they struggled to free themselves the more it would cut into the hide, eventually it would cut a major artery, leaving the beast to suffer a painful death.

He had watched till the sun rays had gone from yellow to orange, and finally a dark red as the sun set below the horizon, the last dark red skies fading, to a darkening ever increasing blackness as the night drew in, before he withdrew and walked back into the lounge.

As he entered, his faithful companion, Mrs. Jay, was sitting in her favorite armchair, before her was the coffee table, neatly laid out, with cups, saucers, coffee percolator together with milk and sugar, and as Bison entered, she too went through her ritual, of carefully turning the bone chine cups over onto the respective saucers, and then gently pouring in the milk, and placing in the respective cups the necessary teaspoons of sugar, before pouring in the coffee.

By this time, Bison had himself settled into his chair, and Mrs. Jay, quietly got up, and picking up one of the saucers on which the cup and teaspoon balanced, walked over and placed this on the coffee table by Bison's side, before returning to her chair and settling down.

Bison, in all the years tried hard not to get caught up in all the latest technology that was available, but had in the past years treated himself to one "luxury," and that was to the owning of a satellite set. Situated where they were, they could not get television reception for the local stations, and if the truth be known, they did not care to do so. For all that, Bison was not one to use the satellite for watching just anything. He enjoyed being able to switch on, and get the News, be it CNN, or SKY, without having to wait till a certain time to get this. He also liked to watch sport too, and of course if there was a nice movie on later, would give in to Mrs. Jay's, asking to watch it!

As he drank his coffee, he raised his left hand to see that it was now approaching 7pm, and that meant that the news would soon be on, so finishing the last sup of coffee, he picked up the television controls, and switched the set on, flicking through to the News programs, and settled down in his chair.

As the headlines were read out, one mention, suddenly had him, and Mrs. Jay, sitting upright- yes- it definitely said that what had been a peaceful march, organized by those who hoped to be the opposition, and eventual winners in the forthcoming elections- IF the elections would ever be held - had been attacked and beaten.

With keen anticipation, they awaited the news on this particular point. When it came, they could not believe their eyes, for there, on the screen, were horrifying pictures, taken from First Street, in Harare (Zimbabwe's capital - which had been called Salisbury - when the country was still known as Rhodesia). Scenes of axe, stick carrying organized bands of "thugs," beating up peaceful marchers. As Bison watched, he saw a "white man" walking up the street, when one of these "thugs" just ran up behind him, and lashed out with his stick- striking the man, who in astonishment turned, and gestured with his hands out - "why?"

The reporter then went on from those scenes, to state not only had Mr. Bugabe, (the countries leader for the past 20 years) once again failed to give a date for the elections to be held, but had also given virtual authority for any such thugs to take over any white owned ranch in the country! This was something that had been ongoing now for some time- and had led to some

900 farms having been forcible taken over by, once again these axe wielding bands of thugs - that Mr. Bugabe called "War Vets", bloody cheek...what an insult to those genuine vets from the World Wars" Bison mused to himself, and in spite of the fact that even the courts had ruled, that these actions were illegal.

As Bison watched, the reporter was shown, out at such a farm- where they had been turned away from the farmstead, as at the gate were a band of axe and machete bearing thugs. As the reporter, withdrew, a few minutes later, the gates were swung open, and heading towards them came a beige Mercedes Benz car- a white male and female occupants therein.

As they approached the reporter, and the pickup, in which he had come to the scene, they stopped, and both, the husband and wife, between sobs, blurted out, how the gang had just come in and given them, 10 minutes to collect whatever they wanted to take with them, and leave! As the reporter was interviewing the family - another vehicle came from the other direction, and in it, was the so called "leader" of this so called "take over" of ranches.

As the reporter went to interview him, he just asked "Is this your ranch "when the reporter stated it was not, the man, held up his hand saying "then I have nothing to say to you." When the reporter tried to follow this up, it was then apparent, that something was amiss, for he was called, and quickly ran back to his pickup, and jumping into this, the driver just managed to pull away from a gang of the so called thugs - that had come from the farmstead, and were now running at them wielding their axes, machetes and sticks, as the pickup pulled away- sticks and stones were thrown after them! These gangs then returned, to throw out all they could find inside the house, and set them on fire. They even set fire to the Farm tractors and Harvesters! So raising the question–Why take over a farm, just to destroy it?

Bison, and Mrs. Jay, exchanged glances - neither could believe what they were seeing. Both knew that for some time now, this so called "take over" had been talked about a lot by Mr. Bugabe - and was recognized as his trying to appease many of those on his side, who had waited for this to happen ever since he had promised this on his gaining power some 20 years ago. At that time- he had said this as a promise, but had realised, that he needed the white farmers, to produce the necessary crops, to help his economy, so had put off his so called promise, every election time he spouted out his promise once again to help him hold on to power–but now, the people of Zimbabwe had realized, that the country under his rule was now become intolerable–food was scarce, fuel was practically unavailable -

which led to a fall in tourism, and all in all the country was now at its worst since the coming into independence! What was once the 'bread basket' for Africa, had now had to resort to begging for food!

As a result of this, Mr. Bugabe knew for a fact that in a fair and free election, there was now every possibility that he would, after 20 years lose the election and his position; the thought of either of these happening were just too terrible for him to contemplate, and he would do anything to stop it– the scenes unfolding, just showed to what lengths he would go to hold onto power!

Bison, turned the television off, slowly raised himself from the chair in which he was sitting, and slowly walked over to the fireplace in which as always there was a nice warm fire burning, crackling sounds coming from the logs as they burnt, the orange and red flames dancing up the chimney.

He paused, and reached out for a framed photograph that was on the mantelpiece.

Bison and Mrs. Jay had had no children of their own, as much as they would have loved to, on many occasions though, especially the one they had now just listened to, and they were both silently glad that they had in fact had none - as that would always add to their worries.

Bison picked up the framed photo - it was an old black and white photo, in it was the portly figure of a man, in the police uniform, the three bars on each epaulet, showing the Section Officer Rank, of the former British South Africa Police (Rhodesia's Police Force), the photo, being in the light over the years, had begun to go a slightly yellow colour, but even so, it was still remarkably clear, and as Bison stood holding the photo, Mrs. Jay had crossed over and stood behind him. They both gazed down at the photo in Bison's hands.

"Aaaah – Tony" Bison said slowly "oh how we wish that you were still here with us now..." he knew that he spoke for both of them, and turning slightly could see the buildup of tears in Mrs. Jay's eyes that she still felt the same.

Although not having any children, they had both, unofficially, adopted Tony - the person in the photo, as their son - in fact they had both, in their wills, cited Tony, as the one to whom they left all three ranches, in the event of their deaths - that's how highly they respected this, Tony Wood.

Tony Wood had been the first, Member in Charge of the police station of Sun yet Sen, some 3-5 miles up the road from the Nazeby Ranch. He and Bison, had shared an amazing relationship over the years that he was at the station. He was always a regular dinner guest at Nazeby– that was way back in the 1960's. That was well before Tony got married to Cheryl, his wife, and prior to his leaving the Police Force.

Bison could still recall the happy occasion of the wedding, to which he and Mrs. Jay had been invited, and following that the joyous news of the birth of Tony's first son, Sean, born in Bulawayo, whilst Tony was at that time a Compound Manager of a gold mine.

Then of course came the sad day, when Tony, Cheryl and son Sean, left to settle in England. They had over the years kept in contact, and had rejoiced with the births of Tony and Cheryl's subsequent children, Barry, Garth, Kirk, Wayne and finally Grant. Photos of each child, yearly or at least every 2-3 years, were constantly sent from Tony and Cheryl to Bison and Mrs. Jay.

Bison let out another sigh and said "Oh yeah, Tony - if only things had not changed - and you were all still here with us...we could certainly do with you now...." and he fell silent, as Mrs. Jay's fingers continued their gentle massage of his neck and shoulders.

Of course the police station, was still up the road, but since the coming of independence, not only had the name of the Police Force changed, but sadly with it - went all the white policemen, and with them went the majority of the "good" African policemen too.

In fact under Tony's time of command, his loyal sergeant major Tazwinga, had for a time assumed command of Sun Yet Sen station, but with the introduction of policemen who were ambitious hungry power seekers, and not at all interested in "policing," he had finally retired, and now had a job, with Bison, as his head of security–based on the Nazeby South Ranch.

This was handy, as Tony could also keep in touch with him, and forward copies of photos when writing to Bison and Mrs. Jay.

Bison reflected, how during Tony's tenure, the Sun Yet Sen police station, stood out in this barren part of the country, like an oasis in the desert, with its luscious green hedge, and grassy areas, mingled with the whitewashed stones. Yet now as you passed the police station, the hedge had all gone, dried up and died, as had the grassy areas. All was barren and dry, with litter all over the once clean and spotless police camp. The coming and going of numerous prostitutes now being a regular sight, as they went in to keep the single, and no doubt some of the married policemen happy!

"What a sad reflection of the times we are now in "mused Bison to himself, as he slowly replaced the framed photo of Tony, back in its pride of place position on the mantelpiece. "Well, my dear, not much we can do about it - just have to wait and see what develops - no good brooding about it...eh? Let's go and have an early night - shall we?" He took Mrs. Jay's arm, and walked off towards the bedroom- with his old but lively mind racing – wondering - just what events would unfold, in these his latter years of life, here in the country that he so LOVED - lived all his life in, built up, and cherished, and were now facing, once again, another uncertain, and even by looks of it bleak and terrorizing future- these latter thoughts he dared not voice to Mrs. Jay-but was sure that similar thought would be crossing her mind this night - "Must drop Tony, a word in the morning" he said more to himself that anything else, but Mrs. Jay heard it, and this time answered "Yes, Dear...although I'm sure he has seen these reports, and is thinking of us now too" she stated. They washed and changed, and wafted off into their own private thoughts, as they drifted off to sleep.

25

Tony got up from his computer in his study, and hobbled out into the lounge where Cheryl sat, knitting. He walked with difficulty due to arthritis, which was in his back and neck, and also affected his hips and legs. The joints were always sore and he had pain down to his calf muscles.

They had been in England twenty three years now, and Tony had had to give up working some 8 years ago - due to his illness. Cheryl too, had Asthma so bad, that she was on four different pumps and a ventilator as well when the situation got bad.

Often when in pain, and when the weather was inclement, Tony would often say "Oh, hell, I don't know, perhaps we should go back to Africa" at which point Cheryl would intercede and say "To what - you would not be able to get a job - what would you do?" Tony would always ponder for a few moments and reply "Aaah, well, I could at least wrap myself in a blanket, sit in the sun, and die - happy and WARM!" and they would both laugh. But deep inside Cheryl knew that, Tony still considered Africa as his home, and missed the way of life and the sun to a large degree.

Oh to be sure, they were content, with what they had here, they had seen their children grow up, the two oldest married, Sean- with Tabitha had presented them with a grandson, Brodie, and then a granddaughter, Karha whilst Barry - with Caroline had presented them with another granddaughter, Sasha, and Grandson, Sebastian.

Tony too had treated himself to the luxury of a satellite - and had now gone over to the digital system, for he too, like Bison, liked to be able to tune into the latest news, whenever he felt like it- without waiting for a set time in the evening to get the latest news. Sport too, he loved to tune into, especially car racing, and cricket, following with keen interest the progress especially of the Zimbabwe cricket team.

How sad he had been, over the 'nightmare' time that the Zimbabawe Cricket Team had been going through, with best players being sacrificed, just so that untalented young black players could fill their places...Tony was not, or had ever been racist, but it was a sad fact that as a result of these changes, even Zimbabwe's Test status was now in doubt!!! What a sad reflection, on what was going on in the country that he so loved.

This day was like any other, as he sat in the lounge, not watching television, but having it on, tuned into the audible side of the programs that he had subscribed to, and especially to the country music- to which he had always been fond of, he raised his left hand and looked at his watch, and then changed the channels on the television, to the CNN News. As the headlines were read out, he suddenly sat up as there was a referral to Zimbabwe and peaceful march that was disrupted. He waited with eagerness till the actual story broke and was all ears as unfolding before him were pictures of the events–in First Street- Harare–scenes he could not believe - people especially whites being singled out for vicious attacks by stick wielding, axe carrying thugs! "Cheryl - are you watching this" he asked, Cheryl had put her knitting down at the break of the story - and nodded "Yeah-what the hell's happening over there?" she stated.

As they watched the news reporter continued onto his coverage of the illegal farm take-overs that were going on- and once again, both Tony and Cheryl could not believe what they saw unravel on the screen before them. "Things are getting worse." Tony exclaimed.

Tony had only the week before phoned his older brother David, who having "retired" from the transport company that he was co director of, had settled in Nyanga (what used to be Inyanga) just north of Mutare (which used to be called Umtali - when the country was Rhodesia), and he had told Tony how the country was in a terrible state - with hardly any fuel available - vehicles being abandoned where they ran out of fuel, David also worked at one of the hotels in the highlands, and as he said with the fuel problems, tourism was virtually nonexistent - with bookings being cancelled as people had no fuel to get up to hotels - in fact he stated that there had been no residents for the past three weeks!

Of course too, David had bought himself a small farm- where he lived, so the events that he had seen on the television, troubled Tony, and more so when he thought of his close friend Bison, who had those three fine ranches, south of Sun Yet Sen - where Tony himself had been stationed back in the 1960s.

The only solace he took was in the fact that his true friend and constant companion from his police career, his ex Sergeant Major, Tazwinga, was now working for Bison, and he knew that Bison would have a true friend, in Tazwinga, but for all that Tony was still troubled by what he had seen going on, and said "Remind me darling, to drop Bison a line - to see how things are really shaping up down there?"

He sat down, again, and looked fondly around the lounge at all the African memorabilia that he had on his wall - all of which brought warm feelings back to him, as he recalled his upbringing, and life in the Africa that he so dearly loved, and yet, filled him with such deep sorrow, when he saw the sad and pathetic state, that was befalling Zimbabwe, and hoped against hope that sense would prevail, that Bugabe would allow the elections, that nearly everyone knew would lead to his losing power, but which Tony also feared would lead to civil war in the country.

"You know, he is a clever old bastard, that Bugabe - I know what he is up to - he is hoping that by his encouraging the takeover of the white's farms, by his gangs of thugs, that one of the farmers - will lose his temper and in defying the gangs, shoot one or more of them - which would give Bugabe - just what he was looking for- a reason to declare a state of emergency- and thus put off the elections for as long as the so called emergency was on for – the crafty blighter" he said out loud, to no-one in particular - as he settled down once again, and turned over the channel, onto the sports channel, and picked up the Nascar racing, in the states, which took his mind off his troubled thoughts for a while. Cheryl who had been sitting calmly by, watching the news and then Tony's reaction, knew though that his thoughts would not really be on the car racing - oh yes it would deviate his thoughts for a short while, but she knew that especially when he retired to bed, that he would not be able to go off to sleep as his thought would travel back to what he had seen, and more than that, he would be worrying just what he could do and how Bison at his age would manage and also how David would cope? - All these questions would race through Tony's mind. He also knew that at the present exchange rate of $8000 to the £1, David could not even think about selling up and coming over to start a new life at age 60 - even if he could sell out - which seemed at this stage - no chance at all, the only thing that Cheryl took comfort from in that regard was the fact that David's farm was really no more than a small holding - but even so with its new dam, the fine main house, and with its second house on the property- it would make an ideal "week-end" retreat for any member of Parliament - so she too had her worries - as she wondered just what the future held for the country of her birth – Rhodesia - or as it was now ZIMBABWE !

26

A month had slowly slipped by, in which Bison had just got on with the work at hand of running three ranches. Even with all the fuel problems, these had not worried Bison too much, for apart from going into Bulawayo to do shopping once a month, he hardly ever used his Landrover, much preferring, even at his present age, to use his horses in going to and fro on farm business.

Mainly it was for by doing so, he could take in the nature of the ranch, be at one with it, and the large amount of wild animals that were on the ranches, ranging from the smallest dik-dik (a small deer) up to and including the largest - elephants!

There was nothing that Bison enjoyed more than riding through the ranch and coming across herds of wild animals, zebra and wildebeests, which always seemed to be found together, and the stately impala, who at his approach, maybe because he was not in a vehicle - did not take fright, as he rode up towards them, but merely parted to let him through as he got nearer- but never the panic, and rushing as they would do, had he been in his Landrover. He just enjoyed studying them, and seeing them run free on his ranches was always a delight to him.

He had been out all day supervising the dipping of the cattle on Nazeby. The weeks before they had dipped all those at Champion Ranch, then next week they would move onto Nazeby South. It was tiresome work, but had to be done, to stop the spread of disease in the cattle, (foot and mouth especially) and to keep the cattle healthy was a prime concern, for it would keep the price right at the forthcoming cattle sales, and one thing that Bison was proud of was his fine herd of cattle.

Of course there were poachers, always had been, and always would be, and he smiled as he recalled in his mind, how it was due to cattle poaching that he had first met Tony. That was way before there was even a police station at Sun Yet Sen, and Tony was but a Constable, stationed at Kezi.

Because of the loss of cattle, he had phoned the Kezi police station, and it was Tony who had come and seen him, and it was a surprise to Bison, when

Tony had asked his permission to spend a couple of weeks on the Champion Ranch, whilst he investigated this problem. Surprise, because it was unusual for a Constable to come all the way down to take a report and then be willing to spend time down on the ranch, which had only a corrugated iron dwelling, approximately 10 feet by 10 feet, which Bison used as his "office," when doing the dipping. There was a bore hole, and pump, so water was plentiful, and there were also the two mud huts, in which his herdsmen and their wives lived - together with their children - but that was all.

He remembered how Tony, had made himself at home, bought a couple of Tilley lights, and tinned food from the nearest African shop in the Sear Block reserve, and how he had spent the two weeks doing extensive searching, and eventual tracking down those responsible, who all pleaded guilty in due time in the Courts and were sentenced to prison sentences. From then on Bison and Tony had become good friends, and of course that friendship grew, even more so when the police station at Sun Yet Sen was opened, and Tony was put in charge of it.

Bison, pulled his horse to a stop, under a large Baobab tree (a distinctive large tree - that looks as though it has been planted upside down - with its large root like branches protruding from its immense thick trunk), and dismounting, tied the reins to the broken branch, and sat down in the shade, pulling out his water bottle, and taking a long cool drink.

He must have sat there for over half an hour, simply doing nothing, just being at one with nature, listening to the sounds, and smelling the smells of the bush, and watching as a pack of baboons wandered by, watching him with interest, as they ambled by, the leader "barking" loudly, and the smallest ones, playing happily, the babies riding on their mothers backs, like jockeys on horses, before he re saddled, and headed leisurely back towards the Nazbey homestead.

It was just going on 4 o'clock in the afternoon, when Bison finally re entered the Nazbey homestead. As he dismounted, a picanin (a young African boy) ran up and took the horse from Bison. "Thank you Jensen" Bison said, as the youngster took the horse towards the stables, and Bison walked into the house.

Mrs. Jay was waiting, dressed as always, in her khaki shirt, and jodhpurs, and she went over and gave him a gentle kiss on the cheeks "How did it go" she inquired, and without waiting for a reply, since from Bison's posture and bearing, she knew that all was well, "I will go and run a bath for you" she sated, and Bison replied "Thank you, my dear " and he headed off to the bedroom to undress, looking forward to a long hot soak, after the tiring day.

Bison was still soaking in his bath, and Mrs. Jay was on the verandah, looking out over the well kept lush lawn, when she noticed a pall of dust, made by an approaching vehicle, as it approached down towards the homestead from the Sun Yet Sen area. As she gazed out towards this, she could eventually make out that there were in fact two vehicles, one following behind the other, and she wondered who on earth would be traveling in convoy, towards them.

The two vehicles travelled down the dirt road from Sun Yet Sen, towards the Nazbey Ranch. The lead vehicle was in fact a Zimbabwe police Landrover, in which sat Inspector Mpofu, who was the current Member In Charge of the Sun Yet Sen police station, and one of his constables was driving, as he sat with his inspector's leather cane, held in his right arm, tapped on the dashboard, his left arm leant out of the window, the wind ruffling his shirt sleeve, and his epaulette, bounced up and down on his shoulder. His peaked cap was pulled low down on his head, and he stared straight ahead, as they bumped down the potted dirt road.

Following behind them was a sleek looking black Toyota sedan. It bore Zimbabwe Government number plates, the driver, was neatly attired in a black chauffeur uniform, right down to the black peaked cap. Sitting behind him, behind the regulatory glass intervening windows, sat a grey haired, distinguished looking African, smartly dressed in a blue safari suit, complete with cravat bearing the Zimbabwe flags, his eyes too were fixed straight ahead, and he had a crooked smile on his face, as though he found what he was doing or about to do, amusing. Next to him on the leather back seat, was a black brief - case. It all looked very official, and ominous.

The convoy continued to trundle down the dry, dirt, dusty road, and finally pulled into the farmhouse vicinity, where they both drew to a halt. The Inspector leapt from his Landrover, and ran over to the black car, upon reaching this; he bent over and opened the back door, and then stood to attention and snapped out a neatly executed salute, as the grey headed man emerged from the car.

Mrs. Jay, was still standing on the verandah, watching all of this, muttering under her breath "Oh- hell, a government official - what the hell's all this about now?" As she stood her ground, the police inspector, followed by this lean statuesque, grey headed government official approached her; the Inspector came to a halt, just in front of her, and without further ado asked "Mr. Pritzkow in?" Mrs. Jay, looked past him to the government official, and said "Yes, he is having a bath at the moment - who shall I say wants to speak to him?" and her eyes fixed on the government official, who held her gaze, and she heard the Inspector reply "The Minister of agriculture, - will you get Mr. Pritzkow–now" it was more of an order than a request, and because of the manner it was said Mrs. Jay responded, by not inviting them in, but saying "Yeah - just wait here, I will go and fetch him for you" as she turned and walked back into the lounge, then on through to the bedroom, where she found Bison already dressed. "Bison- there is that Inspector chappie from Sun Yet Sen - with the minister of agriculture outside to see you" and she felt an uneasiness come over her.

Bison, slipped on his shoes, and said "Damn–did not expect them so soon - oh well let's go and get it over with" and as he started out, Mrs. Jay grabbed his arm "What - do you think it's about farm take-overs" and as soon as she said it, she knew that it could be nothing else- she started at Bison, who broke into a smile, patted her arm and said - "Here now - girl - don't go getting upset yet - let's see what they have to offer," and he walked briskly through the lounge out onto the verandah, and headed, where the two men were standing, still outside the verandah, and he smiled to himself "Well done girlie- you kept them in their place" and he came to a halt just in front of them.

The Inspector, again repeated who the other person with him was, and before Bison could say anymore, the government official spoke "Mr. Pritzkow - Mrs. Jay's bad manners have left us standing out here, I will just come in" he did not wait for an invite and mounted the stairs as he continued" I have a few details to discuss with you - won't take long" and he pushed his way into the lounge, where Mrs. Jay stood.

Bison noticed that he walked with a distinct limp, and just with their so far brief encounter, could feel something very sinister about this man, and yet at the same time, he could be sure that he knew the man, and his mind was racing to see if he could put a name to the face. "Damn it" he said to himself "wish Tazwinga or Tony was here now- they would have placed this chappie already" he was interrupted by the official, who had by this time opened his brief case on the center coffee table, and was pulling out a lot of official looking documents. The inspector stood in the doorway looking on. "You see, Mr. Pritzkow" Bison could pick up immediately, by the way that he pronounced his name, that it was done with a sneer of contempt - "you have three very large ranches - you are old - you just cannot - at your age - manage all of these properly - so to help you out – we - the government - have decided - that we will help you" he said with scorn "by taking one of these from you" as he said this Mrs. Jay gave a gasp, Bison raised his hand to stop her from making any further statement - he could feel that this was a very sinister man, and that with the backing of the official

128

policeman looking on, there was just nothing one could do–so the official went on "all you have to do is sign these papers giving us the right to have one of your ranches" and he had already in his hands the papers, which he set down, and with a quieter voice ordered "just sign, these ...MR...Pritzkow" again there was that absolute contempt in his voice.

Bison, took the forms, and before anything else, let his eyes drop down to where the official had - as he had suspected signed these forms, and immediately he froze...for there...plainly at the bottom of the form was the name NGONGA!

Bison pretended to be pondering over the small print of the forms, as his mind took in the importance of what he had just read - "BASTARD" he whispered to himself, his stomach knotted, and he had to fight to keep his emotions under control, for here in his lounge, giving him these orders was none other than the ex police constable Ngonga who had served under Tony at Sun Yet Sen - had retired, committed a murder, fled the country, returned as a terrorist leader, wiped out the Mambali police post, and then had attacked Bison, when he was at the Nazbey South Ranch, he remembered where he had been shot, and memories of his faithful employee, Toby's wife and son being killed, by this bastard. He drew in a few deep breaths, to calm himself down "bloody hell "he mused to himself" here was the man that Tony had captured, who was sentenced to life imprisonment, and now in this position within this corrupt government," he controlled his feelings, and then he too gave a wry smile, as he thought "I will play you at your own game- you bastard" and then as if having finished reading the documents, and giving not the slightest inclination that he had recognized Ngonga, said "Sure, Minister, I know, as it's for the Government - I will give you my biggest ranch" and as he said this, he filled in the form, and wrote down Champion Ranch as the giveaway "there you are, you can have the Champion Ranch - my biggest ranch "and he signed and gave the papers back to Ngonga, who he saw stop in his tracks, as the horror of what had been done hit him - sure he had been given a ranch - the biggest one at that - but it was well known that, there was nothing on that ranch - that would attract anyone to it - no nice houses, "DAMN" Ngonga said to himself" this old man - has fooled me - I should have killed him those many years ago" but there was nothing he could do right now, although in his devious mind he was already thinking just how he would turn the tables - but for now with the Inspector looking on, he had to accept what he had been given - for after all Mr. Pritzkow had made a big issue of giving the biggest of his ranches to him - he would have to grin and bear it...for the moment.

He snatched the papers from Bison's hand, and walked with a hurried limp, pushing past the inspector, out onto the verandah, and up towards his car - with the Inspector- muttering his "Thank you Mr. Pritzkow - for being so kind" and running to keep up with this sinister - minister. He opened the door for him, and then ran back to his Landrover, jumping in, and by that time the black car was already heading out of the farmyard - so that the Landrover driver had to turn, and follow, but this time not being able to lead - or even keep up with the speedily disappearing black saloon, and the swirl of dust that it left behind.

Mrs. Jay watched as the minister and then the inspector both left, and then turned to face Bison. "Who was that government official?" she inquired. Bison turned and looked at her, and said "Remember, that incident at Nazeby South - when those damn terrorists attacked, and killed Toby's wife and child…" when Mrs. Jay nodded, he continued "…well that bastard, was the ring leader…" he heard Mrs. Jay give a gasp, but continued "…yeah he was the one, that Tony went after and caught down on the Shashe River the bastard got a life sentence for his murder of those poor constables at the Mambali police post, guess he must have been one of Bugabe's right hand men…one of his so called 'war vets'…hell who does he think they are… some kind of heroes…they were bloody terrorists" he paused, to control his shaking anger before continuing…"guess he must have received a pardon…and now…Minister, if you please- in charge of the illegal, unlawful - takeover of farms…." and he stopped and looked at Mrs. Jay, who quickly, but quietly asked "What are we going to do?"

Bison, smiled, and said… "Aaah, well - girlie-at least we have managed to give…alright our biggest of the three ranches, but at least it's the only one on which we have not built on, so they will have to build up on their own and that will cost them. We'll have to wait and see what develops - my only worry is, that if they can - even though the courts have ruled they cannot take over farms, still send a Minister and take over….what's to stop them, from taking our other two as well? "He and Mrs. Jay, just looked at each other, they both knew that this was the case, and at their ages - there was not much that they could do….But ….where could they go?

Bison, walked over to the phone, "At least I can let Tazwinga know" he said, as he picked up the phone, and rang the party line for Nazeby South.

27

Tazwinga was sitting out on the verandah of the fine farmhouse that Bison had rebuilt here at Nazeby South. Of course much of the old house had remained, and with it, often the memories of those dark days - those days when he and Tony Wood, had come to the rescue of Bison, here at this ranch when it had been attacked by terrorists, and how there had been the senseless killing of Toby's wife and child. Tazwinga could clearly recall the incident at if it was just the other day - and the memories of the dastardly deed - not only here, but at the wiping out of the police post at Mambali - by that ex police Constable – Ngonga - would never be eliminated from his mind, and as his thoughts returned, he suddenly got a chill - all over - and it was not just from the fact that the sun had set, no something was not right..."what had brought this sudden 'chill' over me?" he asked himself...but could not find an answer.

As Tazwinga stood up and started to walk slowly back into the house, the phone rang, and he recognized the party line ring- and his pace quickened and he entered through the door- into the lounge, and over to the phone.

"Hello" he said "Tazwinga here" and immediately recognized the sound at the other end "Hiya, Bison...what can I do for you?" he asked.

Bison quickly related the events that had just taken place - there was an eerie silence, as Tazwinga now knew what had caused his sudden 'chill'... the silence was broken at last by Tazwinga who said "That bastard! We should have killed him when we had the chance - damn, Tony and I were too slow - we had him - we could have pretended that he had made a break for it - and shot him - no...that would have been too quick...we should have done to him what he had done to those poor chaps at Mambali" he paused and changing direction went on "you know Bison - he will not want, Champion - oh yeah it's your biggest - but it's got no homestead - nothing that he could make use of..." as he paused Bison said "I know, I just thought I would just get in quick, and get one over him - just to foil him - and frustrate his efforts for a while," he gave a deep sigh and Tazwinga said "Yeah - good try - but he will pull all the strings and try and get Nazeby from you...and then Nazeby South from me too...but not without a fight - and this time I will not hesitate to kill the bastard!" the last two words were uttered with savage contempt, which was picked up immediately by Bison who replied " Yeah - me too Taz - guess we will have to re awaken our anti terrorist teachings- suggest we keep our FNs loaded- and ready old pal - seems like we will end our days fighting all over again..." as he paused Tazwinga cut in "Yeah - like old times - just wish Tony was here too...." he paused and both he and Bison silently, wished for the same thing...Tony to be with them - the trio together again against the old enemy... "Yeah" whispered Bison- "keep a look out old pal - I will let you know if anything else transpires ...." "Watch your back 'old man'" Tazwinga laughingly replied, and Bison laughed and hung up the phone.

After hanging up the phone, Bison slowly walked back towards his study, there behind a large picture of the Victoria Falls, was a cleverly concealed wall safe. Bison pulled out a key, inserting it into what appeared a natural crack in the wall- turned the key, and slowly opened the large door, revealing a large well stocked armory.

Since the forming of Zimbabwe all white farmers had had all their guns confiscated - and were not allowed to carry any form of weapon, except those that were–after very strict scrutiny allowed by the Government - in Bison's case - they allowed him - after a very long heated argument - to possess a shotgun, and a rifle. To this end - Bison had bought a pump action shotgun, whilst in South Africa on a business trip, and had managed to obtain a very old Mk4, 303 rifle - he had over the years stocked up, about 100 times the amount of cartridges he was allowed by law. All these he kept concealed in this cupboard - together with his and Tony's old FN rifles – for which over the years he had on every trip to South Africa built up an abundance of ammunition. Also through contacts in South Africa, he had managed to get a total of fifty hand grenades - which were also carefully stored in this armory, together with two Smith and Wesson .38 revolvers.

He knew the penalty of ever being found with these were immense - but he had always had a niggling feeling - that there might just come the day- that they might be needed- and NOW it seemed- that this just might be the case. Bison surveyed the arsenal that was in front of him, and muttered to himself "What a bloody shame - even at my age - the bastards just won't give up - till they have taken everything ever owned by a white farmer..." he gave a loud sigh and continued. "and then - what do they do - they burn all the crops - throw out all the furniture - computers- set fire to them all - and then just bring in all the cattle they can - and graze the farm areas they take - reducing them in no time to barren wastelands!"

He had just closed the door - and replaced the picture, when Mrs. Jay came in, she called quietly- "Bison - there is a call for you.....it's from England...its Tony..." Bison let out a remarkable cry, that startled Mrs. Jay, and he hurried past her, and into the lounge, to the telephone.

28

When Bison had finished speaking to Tazwinga, Tazwinga slowly walked over to the stable area, he went over to the far corner, and deliberately started to move a large bundle of hay - he was in no hurry - he had hoped that he would never have to come over to this area again.

As he moved the last bit of hay, the cement underneath came into view. Tazwinga walked over to the side of the wooden building - and took a large sledgehammer - and walking back to the cement corner - slowly started to bang on the concrete.

As he did so - the cement slowly cracked - revealing a large square door, Tazwinga continued tapping at the one edge, and the cement crumbled to reveal a lock. He produced a key, unlocked this, and slowly lifted the door which creaked through lack of use, to reveal a large underground vault. He walked back to the side of the building, in an old desk; he pulled open a drawer to reveal a torch - which he took with him back to the vault.

Shinning the torch into the vault, Tazwinga slowly lowered himself down into the dank musky vault. As his feet came to a firm stop, he let go of his hold on the top, and then surveyed the vault.

There in the one corner, was a casket - cautiously opening this, he pulled out two items, carefully wrapped in oilskins. As he opened them, revealed were three FN rifle, and a shotgun - as he shone the torch - he also noticed in the casket - were the large amount of ammunition built up over the years for both of these weapons.

As in the case of Bison - so too with Tazwinga - these were "illegal" weapons - not allowed by law - for all that they had allowed Tazwinga to have was an old .303 rifle!

Tazwinga smiled to himself - as he let his hands reach out and slowly caress the FN rifle that had been with him all through his anti terrorist campaign with Tony, in their police days. "Trusted friend" he said to himself as he held the FN, "how I hoped that I would not have to use you again...but it looks like we are going to be buddies again.." he let out a low laugh "aah, Tony, if only you were here" he mused, and slowly he wrapped them up again, and then pulling himself out of the vault - he closed and locked the door - and slowly moved the hay back over the vault door that was now visible - and only hidden by the hay. Once the hay was in place - he slowly went back to the desk, replaced the torch, and sledge hammer, and slowly walked back to the main building.

The evening was closing in - it was his favourite time of the day - the night noises were starting - jackals baying - crickets chirping - he looked up at the darkening sky - the fresh smell of the night air filled his nostrils - "aah" he muttered to himself "what a wonderful night - what a lovely country that I have been born in - what hell of a mess this damn government has made of it all - and now these bastard so called 'war veterans' - war veterans indeed - damn savage terrorists...who feel they have the right to take whatever they damn well want... well you come and try taking it from me - you will get a surprise - I know I won't win - but hell - I will take a lot of you with me - old as I am" the disdain in his voice was clear, he shook his head sadly, and slowly entered into the main building again.

29

Tony waited patiently as he heard Mrs. Jay call to Bison, and heard his whoop of delight, and in a few moments the old man's voice came through clear as a bell "Hiya Tony - how are you?" he inquired and after Tony had brought him up to date with what was going on in England, he hesitantly asked "What about your end, Bison? I have been watching the news - can't believe what I am seeing - what the hell is happening over there - has no one any sense left at all?" he left the question hanging- not expecting an answer, then gravely asked " will you all be O.K.? Any signs of anyone trying to take your farms from you?" and went deathly quiet, as Bison revealed what had taken place.

When Bison got to the point where he mentioned Ngonga's name, the hairs on Tony's neck bristled, he cut in "The bastard- so that's what became of him...eh...crafty swine...yeah I can just see him trying to grab your farms..." he paused, and with deep concern in his voice continued "Bison, old pal, please be very careful - that Ngonga's a snake - he won't be satisfied with Champion Ranch he will want it all - especially Nazeby..." he paused again, then asked " does he know that Taz is at Nazeby South?" Bison replied that he did not think so, and then went on to tell Tony that both he and Taz had stored up an armory for just such an occasion, and Tony cut in once again "Yeah Bison, but you be careful - not only because of the dangers if you are known to have these weapons but also- hell you can't hold them all off." before he could continue, Bison gave a chuckle and said "No that's true, Tony, but hell I will go down taking many with me - and my first shot will be on... you know who...heck with Taz by my side, it will be like old times - sorry you could not be besides us too" he went quiet for a while - then continued "but who knows - it might not come to anything - will have to wait and see - Ngonga will have to pull some mighty strong strings to get all of the farms - especially as I have given him the biggest - and South is owned and run by an African. Anyway so much of this morbid stuff - how are you and all yours?" he inquired, and Tony brought him up to speed on all the news about the welfare of his family - and then ended the call.

Replacing the phone, Tony turned to Cheryl - and gave her all the news from Bison–she too blanched when she heard that Ngonga was now in the position to take people's farms- legally with the blessing of Bugabe!

"Oh, Tony "she muttered "what will become of them...they are both so old, Bison and Mrs. Jay - Taz himself no youngster same age as you...." before she could go on Tony interrupted "Thanks...Sweetheart...how encouraging to hear me placed on the geriatrics list..." and Cheryl's retorted "silly...you know what I mean - you're not as fit and able as you were back then darling."

Tony crossed to the lounge door- looking out at the night sky- he muttered slowly "we will just have to wait and see...but that swine Ngonga... I know him...damn, I should have finished him when I had the chance...but then, someone else would have been given the same job...no going against that Bugabe, and his so called 'war vets'...they are not war veterans...they are no more than terrorists, always will be "and without more ado - he stepped out into the small garden off the lounge. Cheryl let him go...she knew how troubled he would be, and knew that he just had to see it out...no matter how long it took. She vividly remembered the nightmares that Tony suffered over the dastardly deeds of Ngonga at Mambali police post...and how these had plagued Tony ever since. It pained her to see him in such distress, over what was going in a country that he loved, and served all those years ago. Her gaze automatically went to the shelf whereupon stood the Mug and Tankard given to Tony when he had resigned, and the picture frame that Tony had made, containing his old, Cap badge, Shoulder flash, and rank bars...of the BSAP, Rhodesia's Police Force.

30

It was a fine bright Monday morning, and after a hearty breakfast, Bison as was his habit over the years- was off to Nazeby South to watch as the dipping was done, he knew that Tazwinga always could manage, but he enjoyed the trip and looked forward to staying the night with his old pal Tazwinga, and how they could sit for hours discussing the past - something that Bison was never tired of doing.

He had given Mrs. Jay, a kiss, and had already sneaked out his FN rifle into the Landrover; he did not want her to see it, for she would just worry. Mrs. Jay watched and wondered why he was taking the Landrover, as he had always ridden down before, but did not question him.

He opened the door - and jumped into the driver's seat of his old Short Wheeled based Landrover. He put the key in the ignition, turned it and the engine fired first time. Engaging gear, he slowly pulled out of the ranch house area, waving happily to Mrs. Jay and off onto the road that led to Nazeby South, a trail of dust followed him, as he went down the dry dirt road. As he got out from the ranch area, he reached down and slid out his FN rifle, and pulled it up on the seat next to him, it was already loaded and cocked, with the safety on..." Just in case " he muttered to himself, for although it had been six months since Ngonga had visited him, and three months since the Champion ranch was officially taken off him, and given to a band of so called 'war vets,' Bison had always been uneasy about what lay ahead.

He came to the Shashani River, which was down to a trickle - due to the drought, and slowed and came to a stop, at the iron gate that formed the boundary between Nazeby and Nazeby South Ranches.

He got out and calmly walked towards the gate, which was surrounded on both sides by bushes and trees, and as he went to open the old rusty bolt there was a sudden rush and a bloodcurdling yell "Die you old imperialist dog" and three Africans came from out of the bush, with pangas (a traditional African weapon about two feet long - used to cut down trees) and knobkerries (another traditional weapon - a club made from solid wood - narrow - about two to three feet long, with a bulbous head) in their hands, as they rushed at Bison.

Bison was taken by complete surprise...he swivelled round to meet them, his left hand automatically coming up to protect his face - as one of the pangas swung at his head - the panga, cut into his tough - old arm, cutting deep down to the bone, he swung round, gritting his teeth, ducking down, and charging like a bull elephant, at the one wielding the panga, catching him off guard, and throwing him to the side, he ran back to his Landrover.

As he reached it, the other two, had caught up with him, and were raining blows with their knobkerries onto his back and feet, as Bison, leaned inside, and gripped his FN with his only good hand, his right, as his hand slid up, it automatically slid the safety catch off, he kicked back on the door - which sent one of the two intruders, flying backwards, and then, without hesitating, he let off a burst of shells, that tore into the other intruders stomach, throwing him back, legs akimbo, as he fell screaming, holding his hands to his stomach to try and stop the flow of blood, a surprised look on his face and, his screams cutting off in mid sentence he died. The other two having witnessed the death of their comrade - disappeared as fast as they could into the brush, as Bison sprayed a further burst in their direction - being a hunter, he heard the familiar 'thud' as he heard bullet strike skin, followed by an eerie howl, and he knew that he had hit at least one more of them." Good you bastard, hope you take a long time dying, and in agony too "he muttered.

His left arm was hanging limply, blood pounding forth with each heartbeat he took- and he instantly took off his belt, placed it with his right hand over the broken bloody left arm, near the shoulder, and pulled as tight as he could, to reduce the flow of blood. His heartbeat was already pounding in his head, and he felt dizzy- and knew that he had already lost a lot of blood... "Must get to Taz" he said, and jumping back into the Landrover, he put it into first gear, and crashed through the steel gate, and bounced down into the river.

The crossing was made harder, by his having only the one good hand, but he made his way across, and knew that the dip, was just a short way ahead "Damn," he muttered "what a fine mess...how the hell did I not see them. I must be getting old." He mused as the Landrover still in first gear laboured its way down towards the dipping area of Nazeby South.

31

Tazwinga had risen, as always, early this Monday morning. It was a lovely bright day- that by five the sun had already cast its first rays over the far hills, and the light cast through the fine tall tree that encompassed Nazeby South Ranch. The dawn chorus from the birds was well under way; by the time that Tazwinga had emerged from the building, and had walked over to the garage where the old Willis Jeep was housed.

Into the back he threw a bundle that he had carried from the main house, it was his 'lunch' - simple as always consisting of a few sandwiches, and two bottles of cold Fanta orange juice. As these landed he turned and walked over to the old stable area, entering the building, he moved two bundles of hay, and swung open the large square door that was under these, and sank down into the dank vault, crossing over to the casket, removed his FN rifle from its oilskin, and reached around in the dark, and found the double clip of ammunition which he clicked into place, before closing the casket, and making his way to the feint light coming through the open doorway, and pulling himself clear, closed the creaking door, and replaced the bundles of hay over them. "Now what in hell made me do that" he said to himself, "it's been months since them terrorists legally occupied Champion Ranch, and no trouble so far..." he paused, then as he continued his walk towards the jeep said "Oh well, I suppose it's better to always be on the alert" and on reaching the jeep, slid the FN underneath the seat.

He knew that the farm workers, would already be up at the dipping area, just short of the Shashani river, and that they would be waiting for him, and the arrival of Bison, who always attended this dipping, and spent the night at Nazeby South, where he and Tazwinga, had a lovely evening recalling past days - and would always get round to the mention of their dear friend Tony Woods, who was now settled in England.

He jumped into the Jeep, and after firing it up, drove casually up the road, past the homestead, and into the wilderness leading to the dipping area.

He arrived at the dip, at just after 7am, and was glad to see that all the cattle had been assembled, and were herded in the large pasture - enclosure that was on the south end of the dip. Leading out from this, was a narrow fence way at the moment the entrance to this narrow entrance was 'guarded' by three thick beams, to prevent any of the cattle getting through. When ready one of the herdsmen would withdraw this and the dipping would commence.

He pulled to a stop, and walked over to greet the herdsmen, who as always, were pleased to see him and catch up with all the latest news, since their last encounter, and to tell on how the cattle were doing.

It was whilst there was a pause from their talking, that each was reflecting on the day ahead, that Tazwinga, and the others suddenly heard it. It was a burst of gunfire! Tazwinga immediately recognized it as having come from a FN rifle, and his blood ran cold. He knew that only Bison had an FN. He jumped to his feet- told the herdsmen, to commence the dipping, that he would be back, and ran to the jeep. As he got into this, he heard another burst, and realized that it came from up the road, towards the Shashani River, and he knew that it could only have come from Bison.

"Oh no" he thought "they have ambushed him!" as he started the engine of the jeep, he pulled out his own FN, cocked this and applied the safety catch, and then pulled away from the dip, heading towards the Shashani River area, in a cloud of dust, praying that his good friend Bison would be O.K. till he could get to him.

32

The two 'war vets' (terrorist's) had run into the thicket, after their attack on Bison, after seeing their comrade shot down and killed, and could not believe that a white farmer possessed an automatic weapon - THEY were the only ones that had permission to keep their AK47 assault rifles, carefully concealed - in their case, back at the Champion Ranch.

As they ran, they heard a burst of rifle fire, and then one of the two let out a yell, as several stray bullets, tore through his clothes, piercing his back, and killing him. The last remaining terrorist, stopped briefly - on seeing his friend dead, leapt through the underbrush, heading back to Champion Ranch, where the other terrorists would all be waiting to hear of their killing this white farmer.

As he arrived at the Champion Ranches only building, a corrugated iron shack, he was greeted by the others that were duly waiting for his arrival, and were dismayed to see just one of the three, but assumed that the other two had already taken up occupancy of the two new farms.

Their smiles quickly diminished when their comrade explained just what had happened, and they needed no urging, to take out their concealed weapons, and immediately joined their comrade, as they went in search of this white farmer, who they now just had to kill once and for all.

Leaving just one of their comrades behind, they immediately set off once more, out towards the Nazeby South Ranch, where they thought that Bison would be heading to.

Although taking with them their AK 47 assault rifles, they also made sure that they each carried with them, their pangas and knobkerries, for they were also aware that their supreme commander, Ngonga, had instructed them carefully, about the re possession of farms, telling them that they must only use their rifles if the farmers opened fire first, so they could justify their use, but otherwise to only use their brutal force, with their pangas and knobkerries to beat them and cut them down. They were convinced now that Bison had opened fire on them, that they were within their right to take their weapons and now 'legally' finish him off.

Bison slowly guided his Landrover, up out of the Shashani river, the pain from his mangled left arm was excruciating, he had to really concentrate, as without his left arm, his right hand was steering, and he was unable to change gears, so the Landrover was proceeding in low gear only, but his dizziness from the loss of blood, and from the force of the attack on a man of his age was beginning to take its toll, he was having to fight to keep control, not only of the Landrover but also of his falling into unconsciousness.

He saw another steel gate ahead, and he accelerated, so that the Landrover would crash through the gate, but on doing so, the jarring was severe and sent waves of severe pain washing over him, and he nearly blacked out..." Must keep going" he mused to himself..." must make it to Taz..." and he momentarily left the steering wheel, and changed the gear with his right good arm into second so that now he could speed up.

As he fought to keep himself from lapsing into unconsciousness, he struggled to keep his eyes on the rough dirt road, as the Landrover increased speed, and as he turned a corner, he saw down the road ahead, something approaching him, he peered harder, and then could make out that it was another vehicle, the tell-tale cloud of dust from behind it confirmed this, and his spirits began to rise "Can only be Taz...he must have heard the shooting, and coming to investigate.." he muttered, as he slowed the Landrover down, and gradually bringing it to a stop, he switched off the motor, and slumped over the steering wheel.

*****

Tazwinga, gunned the old Willis jeep, down the bumpy dirt road towards the Shashani River, from where he had heard the gunfire coming, his adrenalin was pumping. He turned a corner, and down the straight road, his heart leapt for joy, for there, coming towards him, was Bison's Landrover, and he knew that Bison was O.K.

But as he approached, he saw the Landrover slow down, and pull the side and stop, and suddenly his instincts took over again, his years of terrorist training, came into play, and immediately, expecting the worse, that the Landrover could in fact be driven by terrorists and not Bison at all, he too, pulled the jeep over into the thicket - bumping and crashing through the undergrowth, he pulled the jeep to a stop, and switched off.

He automatically grabbed for his FN rifle, as he jumped from the vehicle, and slid down into the bushes.

He waited for what seemed like an eternity, but was in fact just a few minutes, listening intently, but hearing no sounds of any encroaching footsteps, he slowly began to edge himself forwards, crawling, sliding on his stomach, towards the road, and the Landrover.

The nearer he got, he could suddenly see that there appeared to be only one occupant in the front, and that he could clearly now see was none other than Bison, but still cautious, as to the possibility of an ambush, he continued to approach, through the bushes, slowly as he could, till he was now, right opposite the Landrover, and could see Bison slumped over the steering wheel. His heart missed a beat... "Hope he is not dead..." he said to himself in a whisper. Then gathering himself up slowly, he sprang from out of the bushes, and ran up to the side of the Landrover - there was no attack forthcoming, and he then realised that Bison was in fact on his own, and he immediately, opened the door, reached in, and moved Bison slowly back from his slumped over position on the steering wheel, as he did so, his left arm came into contact with Bison's own left arm, hanging loosely, and the blood, could be seen, and the shock, of what he saw, made him jump - he was used to seeing death and destruction, but was just not prepared to have seen this "What have the bastards done" he exclaimed, as he gently lay Bison back, he gave a slow subdued cry of pain, opened his eyes, even in his pain, he managed a grin, on that craggy old face of his..." Hey Taz...what took you so long..." he stopped coughed, which had him in pain again, then continued " they were waiting at the gate for me...must be getting old...or too complacent...did not expect them or see them till too late. Taz...won't they ever be satisfied...the more you give the more they want eh?" He was just so frustrated with the way things were going in his beloved Africa. Tazwinga, moved Bison slowly over to the passenger side of the Landrover, and then getting into the Landrover, started it up, and started back down towards where he had come from, the dipping area.

Arriving at the dipping area, the herdsmen came running up, and they too were shocked at what they saw, these were men that had served Bison, ever since he had been farming in this area - 50 years, of love for a fair man showed in their immediate reactions, "We have our pangas, and knobkerries – let's go get the ones who did this bad thing..." they yelled but were interrupted by Tazwinga, who said "No...Go back to your homes...lie low, for sure they will be coming back, and they will only take it out on you, for being Mr. Pritzkow's loyal ones...so no...go back to your homes...it's a sad day, that we fellow Africans born here, have to witness such sadness, in this our beloved country...hamba gashle (go in peace)" he added, as they each slowly came forward and wished Bison their best, and he smiled back at them, and thanked them through his pain, and after the final one left, Tazwinga got back into the Landrover and Bison turned and said "Take me home Taz" and they headed back to the Nazeby ranch house.

33

The journey back to Nazeby took longer than expected, it was because Tazwinga was aware that every bump in the road, added to Bison's pain, although aware at the same time, that the bleeding was so severe, and Bison was nearing passing out, he tried to go as fast as he dared.

At last the homestead came into view, and as he approached the house, he gave three short blasts on the hooter; it was an old practice that everyone knew heralded 'danger'!

As the three short blasts from the hooter rang out, Mrs. Jay, who was reading in the lounge, stopped immediately, her heart to her mouth, "What...what could the matter be" she said to herself, as she walked briskly to the door.

As she got into the garden, and into the open area, she found that already all the African staff, both household, and workers, were already gathered round the Landrover, the African women were already uttering their painful moans, and Mrs. Jay knew right away, that someone was badly injured, and automatically imagined that it must be Tazwinga, and that Bison had brought him back to the home.

She quickened her pace, and as she approached, the crowd of loyal Africans, slowly parted, allowing her freedom of passage, averting their eyes from even looking at her, she was then sure that there was something very seriously wrong.

She got up to the Landrover, and immediately saw Tazwinga standing by the side of it, and she caught her breath, as it suddenly now dawned on her, that now the only other one it could be was her beloved Bison.

She cast a look at Tazwinga, and hurried her last few steps, and as Tazwinga opened the door, to reveal Bison's dreadful injuries, the shock was just too great for this fine, cultured old lady, she was shaken so badly by what she saw, that her frail old heart could not take the shock and succumbed to a massive heart attack and died, falling into Tazwinga's arms.

Bison stirred, as through his blurred vision he had witnessed what had just happened, and turning to Tazwinga, said "Taz, take her into the main bedroom please...old pal." After this had been done Bison continued "Take me in please, Taz" and Taz did just that.

Once back inside the house, old Bison's head cleared, it was as if he had found inner strength from somewhere, just when needed most, he sat on his armchair, and said "Taz, take these keys and open the safe, and bring me, the two envelopes - the large brown ones please" Tazwinga took the keys from his pal, and went over, opened the safe, and found the two envelopes, and duly brought these over to Bison.

Bison, gathered himself up, and reaching over to the side table, grabbed a pen, and opened the two envelopes, as he did so, he said to Taz "please phone the Sun Yet Sen police station - speak to Inspector Mpofu and ask him to please come down as soon as he can - stress the urgency - say I've had a bad accident..." he stopped and Tazwinga was already on the phone, after a brief conversation, turned and said "He is coming straight away," Bison smiled, and returned to the official looking papers in front of him.

It took Inspector Mpofu just fifteen minutes to reach the Nazeby homestead. He came briskly up to the lounge door, knocking, and waiting for Bison to wave him in.

As he entered he saw Bison's injuries, and was taken aback..." What on earth happened "he inquired, and Tazwinga, immediately responded, "He got caught in the plow- harvester, I only just got him out on time" the Inspector seemed to accept this, as Tazwinga went on "Poor Mrs. Jay, suffered a massive heart attack at the sight of this, and has died" the Inspector immediately leant forward towards Bison and muttered "I am deeply sorry to hear of her death, she was a fine well liked woman." Bison nodded acceptance of his condolences, then turning to look at the Inspector, said, "Please, please, sit down, I have some very important papers that I want you to witness for me" Mpofu said "Of course Mr. Pritzkow, delighted to assist."

At this Bison took the papers, and offered them to Inspector Mpofu to read. They were firstly his last will and testament, in which he clearly stated, that his Nazeby South Ranch, he did this day, leave to his loyal trustworthy friend, Tazwinga, and that in the event of his death, his Nazeby Ranch, was left to his loyal and faithful Toby!

Inspector Mpofu, was noticeably shaken by what he had read, yet at the same time, his admiration for Bison showed too, as he realized that this grand old man, was leaving his entire ranches, to AFRICANS! He read on, and duly fixed his signature, to the document, after Bison had signed in his presence, and Tazwinga signed too.

Then he produced the deeds for both ranches, and again added his conceding these over to those indicated in his will, again had both Tazwinga and Inspector Mpofu, witness them. As the Inspector finished doing so, he looked at Bison and said "But I am sure Mr. Pritzkow, that if we hurry you through to Bulawayo - with emergency help, you will still be round for a while yet, sir." Bison, turned his wise old head, and looking the inspector in the eye said "Aaah, alas, these old bones, and heart, don't foresee that, I'm afraid, I think it is, alas, too late..." and without having time to say anymore, he rolled over back into his chair, his old craggy face, in a smile, and before all those in the room he too quietly passed away.

34

After Inspector Mpofu had left, Tazwinga got onto the phone, called England, and got through to Tony.

Tony was sitting in his study at the time that the call came through, Wayne answered the phone, and was puzzled, then bringing the phone over to the study was met by his mother, Cheryl who inquired "who is it Wayne?" Wayne replied, "I think he said he was 'Tazwinga'–calling from Zimbabwe..." and before he could finish, Tony had taken the phone from him. "Thanks Wayne" he said, and he and Cheryl exchanged glances, they both knew that it was not often that Tazwinga phoned, and they both feared the worst.

"Hiya Taz - you old skellum (rascal) – to what do I owe this privileged call..." and before he could continue, Tazwinga cut in and passed on the news on the death of his pal Bison, and that of Mrs. Jay.

Cheryl's who was standing in the doorway, saw the sudden change in Tony's expression, the whitening of his fingers as the grasped the phone more tightly, as the full account of the savagery that had befallen Bison was told him, Once the call was over, Tony handed the phone back to Wayne who took it back to the lounge. Tony slowly turned to Cheryl and said "The bastards, have killed Bison, set upon him as he was opening a gate, ...Mrs. Jay, died with a heart attack, when Taz, brought Bison home...hell that's what Bugabe's so called 'war vets' are about... Cheryl, just what the hell is Africa coming to, can't anyone with any sense see, that it's discrimination in reverse now...if you're white...your life's not worth a thing anymore...can't others see what a state the country has deteriorated to...tell you what, if there had been oil, in Zim, by now England and USA, would have been in, guns blazing, and taken out this despot Bugabe...! He stopped, not knowing what else to say for a while.

"BUT" he continued, "Old Bison got the last laugh in the end. He had the guts and will to change both his will and deeds of both Nazeby and Nazeby

South, giving them to Taz and old Tobi..." he laughed through the sadness, and continued "He even got Inspector Mpofu from Sun-Yet-Sen, to officially witness the change over, and had copies sent to the District Commissioner's Office, and Agriculture Minister, that weasel...Ngonga..." he virtually spat out the last name. "What I would have given to see his face...when he realized that those two ranches are now owned by Africans, he can no longer claim these for his so called war vets..." and he chuckled to himself again.

Inspector Mpofu, on leaving Bison the night he had died, had taken all the papers, photocopied them, returning the originals, sending the duplicates to the District Commissioner's Office, and Agricultural Department, so showing that now all of these three ranches in this area, were now all controlled and run, by indigenous African peoples, thus securing them from any further attempts of seizure by the so called "war vets." Ngonga was heard to beat his fists on his desk for hours after receiving this news - but everyone knew that although he had lost this one, there were many other farms in the Matabeleland district that he could set his eyes on.

35

Days after the death of both Bison and Mrs. Jay, Tazwinga had arranged their burial, in the garden in front of the Nazeby ranch, which was attended by all the workers and Inspector Mpofu too. Tony and Cheryl had sent their condolences, and cards, but were unable to make the trip.

Tony had sat quietly in his armchair, on the day that Bison and Mrs. Jay's funerals were held, in a token of respect, and sadness at the passing of his real good pals. Cheryl had noticed it, and had let him well alone with his thoughts. Their oldest son, Sean, back from serving in Afghanistan, with the Royal Engineers, was up for the weekend - and Cheryl had told him what had transpired.

Tony looked up, and seeing Sean in the doorway, stood up and walked slowly up to him, they both embraced, and without saying a word, for both knew what the other was thinking at this sad time. Sean and the other children had often heard numerous stories involving their dad, Bison, Tazwinga, and Ngonga.

Tony stood for a while, then turning to Sean said "Son, call Mum into the room please" Sean looked at his dad, saw the look in his eyes, a look he had seen in the eyes of his Comrades, when a fellow member had been killed in battle, it was that look of determination, to avenge the death. He turned to get his mother.

When Cheryl came back into the lounge, with Sean, Barry, Garth, Kirk Wayne and Grant were in tow. As they were all in, Tony looked up, and quietly said "I am going to Zim - to see Tazwinga." Cheryl froze - and a chill went over her, there was something in Tony's voice, which brought back memories of the violent times he had been through. Before she could say anything, Sean spoke up "I have a month's leave due to me - I will go with you Dad" as soon as he had said so the other lads also stated that they all would go. Tony held up his hand, they stopped and listened as he said 'Thanks, Lads, it means a lot to me that you all want to go with me, but NO, I would rather you stay with your Mum. Sean has had his Army training - and of course his time in the battlefronts of Afghanistan, so he would not need any ' training', to know how to respond to a situation, should it arise." Cheryl interjected "But, Sweetheart- your age and arthritis would you be able to get about..." and before she had finished - Tony replied "You all recall, when we went to Lanzarote for a holiday - how the very next day - and for the rest of our 2 week stay - I managed to walk without my stick, even line dancing in the evenings - so I think too, in Zim with its temperature - I will be as agile as a goat", be it an old goat!!!

Cheryl had to agree, and though troubled in spirit, knew that Tony would not stop till he had been over to see Bison and Mrs Jay's grave - and to see both old Tobi and Tazwinga. "I'm sure that he would not get up to anything too dangerous" she mused to herself yet she had the feeling that there was more to this 'visit' and grave apprehension came over her.

Two days later, Tony called Tazwinga in Zimbabwe.

Tazwinga was sitting on the verandah, as usual, when he heard the telephone ring. He got up wondering who would be calling him, and strolled inside. He picked up the phone and said "Tazwinga' who's calling?" and his face suddenly came alive, "Tony...hey great to hear from you" then fearing something might be wrong, his tone changed "Nothing the matter, is there?" Tony explained the nature of his call, and Tazwinga's grin widened 'Of Course, it would be great to see you, in fact it would be a fantastic boost to all those here, on both ranches, and the area as a whole to see you once more, give me the date of your arrival and flight number, and I will drive through to Bulawayo Airport to meet you," and as he listened, Tony gave him all the details.

36

Tazwinga had risen from his sleep that Morning, he dressed, and after having a wash and some breakfast, walked out to where his Jeep was parked. The jeep had been given to him by Bison, when Tazwinga accepted the job of 'security manager' of the ranches. He paused as he passed the shed, and then quickly returned to the house, and going over to his 'firearms cabinet' took out the .303 Rifle, which was the only gun that he was allowed by law to carry. Taking it out, together with some cartridges, he walked back out to the Jeep. Behind the driver's seat he had secured a steel box, which he now unlocked, opened and housed the .303 Rifle 'Better this than nothing' he mused to himself. He then started the old Jeep, and drove off toward Nazeby Ranch.

As Tazwinga pulled into Nazeby, there was old Toby, who had been given the ranch on the death of Bison and Mrs. Jay. He waved his frail old hand, as he saw Tazwinga approach. As the Jeep pulled to a stop, he shook hands with Tazwinga and asked "Where are you off to?" Tazwinga told him where he was going, Toby's old craggy face, lit up immediately when he heard that 'Ndlovu' was coming. "Here" he said, taking Tazwinga by the arm "Take the Landrover, it does a few more miles to the gallon, than that old Jeep" he laughed, and Tazwinga was grateful for the gesture, for indeed petrol was at a premium in the country, and to have a vehicle that would go further on the petrol they were allowed, or could get, was indeed, most welcome. "Thanks Toby," Tazwinga said "appreciate it" and he undid the lock and slid the .303 Rifle and cartridges out, and wandered over to the Landrover. It was Bison's old favorite, and also contained a steel box to house weapons, which he unlocked, and re housed the .303 Rifle. He jumped in, and as he had expected, as he turned the switch, the tank registered FULL. He knew that this would be so, for Toby never used the Landrover, but took care to always have it full, in case he or Tazwinga needed it. He thanked Toby once again, and then drove off, up the road, towards Sun Yet Sen, then Kezi, Matopos and finally into Bulawayo.

Passing through Bulawayo, he took the road that went out towards the airport, and finally arriving, parked the Landrover, and strolled into the airport. He went up to the lounge, and after ordering a Lion Lager, he went out to the balcony, secured a seat, and waited for the plane carrying Tony to arrive.

Tony and Sean had flown out by South African Airways, to Johannesburg, and then got a connecting flight, through to Bulawayo in Zimbabwe. As the plane circled prior to landing, Tony was peering out of the window, he noticed how dry and parched the landscape appeared Obviously no rain for some time,' he mused to himself.

The plane touched down, on the tarmac runway, and finally came to a halt. As Tony and Sean came out onto the 'stairway' from the plane, the bright sunlight, and heat hit them, and Tony reached for his' wrap round' dark glasses, and slipped them over his glasses, they continued towards the Airport building, and as they neared, he heard a shout "NDLOVU...Tony - up here" both Tony and Sean looked up, and immediately, Tony picked out, his friend Tazwinga, he waved, and shouted back "See you inside Taz" as they walked into the Customs and Immigration posts at the airport.

The Immigration Official, looked at their British passports, and said "business or pleasure visit...Mr. Wood?" looking straight at Tony.

"Pleasure, of course" replied Tony, "looking up old friends." The Immigration Official, studied Tony for a while longer, but could not hold the stare from Tony for much longer, and concentrated on looking over the passports and the completed forms, that both Tony and Sean had handed over, he then stated "Not much down in the area you are going" to which Tony replied "Only the place where two good friends were recently buried, and some old, dear friends still live." The Immigration Official grunted, then stamping both passports stated "Over to Customs, please," and turned to deal with the next person, as Tony and Sean, ambled over to the Customs Counter.

The Customs Officer, after asking how long they were in the country for asked to see their luggage - and after opening both suitcases - and searching through, without finding anything suspicious, asked for their hand luggage. Tony had, made good use of the chance to purchase three, duty free bottles of brandy, the Custom Officer, immediately, on seeing these said " Aaah, I presume, two for you, and one for me eh" in a joking manner, but with undertones that Tony immediately picked up, and to which Tony responded in a quiet whisper "Well, of course," the Customs Officer, was taken aback for a second or two, and then as quick as a flash, grabbed the one bottle, and hid it under his desk, saying "Everything in order here Mr. Wood, do enjoy your stay in Zimbabwe," and with that they were ushered through, and were soon in the lobby, where Tazwinga was waiting for them.

*****

As they saw each other, Taz and Tony, hurried forward, and embraced, having given the traditional 'African handshake first. "Goodness Taz, it's so good to see you after all this time, you have hardly put on an ounce - but wow look at that grey hair!" Tony chuckled, and Taz stood back, looking at his old pal, and said "Yeah, been a while eh–seems like time has not been so good to you though" as he noticed the walking stick in Tony's left hand "and your hair, has almost gone" he laughed. Tony introduced Sean, and they slowly walked out of the Airport, over to where Taz had parked the Landrover. His eyes automatically noticed the 'weapons box,', Tazwinga caught his glance and said "only allowed to carry a .303 Rifle–but I and Toby do have some others concealed" he said, and Tony grinned "Thought you would, Taz," as they all boarded the Landrover.

They got into this and drove from the airport into Bulawayo. Tony could not help but notice that, at the airport there had been very few cars, and on the trip into Bulawayo, if they passed more than three vehicles, that was a lot! "Mmmm," he mused to himself" just as Dave had said, petrol was in short supply." He also noticed how dry and arid it was, and knew that the area had not had much rain either.

They stopped off at Greys Inn, in Bulawayo for a beer and a toasted steak sandwich, and fond memories came back to him, for it was here that he and Cheryl had held their after-wedding drinks. They had earlier got married at the registry office, with Tony's sister and brother in law present as witnesses, and then had returned to their individual work places, with Tony breaking the news to his mates, who did not believe him at first, till he produced the marriage certificate! Then that evening they all met at Greys Inn, for some drinks, and then later Tony and Cheryl proceeded to the Calabash Steak House, for a meal, and serving there was the man who was going to be the best man, and he seated them at a table, whereupon Tony old him that they were married that afternoon...John did not believe it either, till he saw the marriage license, and then bewailed "Thanks, I had just bought myself a suit for the occasion too!" Tony smiled to himself at the memories, and then went and using the public phone, put a call through to his brother David.

David was sitting in his verandah, on his Smallholding (which he had at last managed to sell to a storeowner in Mutare, and had bought a bungalow in Borrowdale) , looking down onto the fine Dam that he had erected, when his wife Maureen, came to him and said "There is a call for you...from Tony...it's ever so clear" as she handed over the phone to David. David took the phone and said "Hello Tony, how's it going?" Then after Tony had explained where he was, said "What the heck you doing back here?" Tony very briefly ran through all that had transpired, and David said "Well, Tony, if you like, I can come and give you a hand...I am due some leave from the Hotel in Umtali, and as you know, with my numerous call-ups during the war years, had reached the rank of Sergeant...so can handle myself, be it may be a bit slower now" Tony thanked him after obtaining his new phone number, and said that he would phone him later.

As the call finished, and the beers too, they went back outside and started to drive off, Tony again noticed that in those wide streets, there was again very few vehicles, and also noticed how 'dirty' the streets were, littered with rubbish He sighed, as he could see how the beautiful big streets were now a collection of rubbish, "Why, oh why- what a waste" he mused to himself.

The drive from the Airport, back down to Nazeby was uneventful, he pointed out as they passed Matopo, to Sean, the spot where Cecil John Rhodes, was buried, Sean recalled that he had been the founder of what was then Rhodesia. Sean also noted the wild life that was in evidence, along the side of the road, zebra, sable antelope, and impala, it was a fantastic sight to be able to see these, first hand as it were, in their natural environment, and noted how both Tazwinga and his dad, Tony, just took it all in their stride, for them it was just accepted, that these would be here, in the country that they both loved so. They drove on and Sean noticed how the road had changed, from a normal wide tarmac road, to what was now just a strip, down the middle of the road. If another vehicle came towards them, both would pull off from the tarmac strip, so that two wheels would be in the dirt on the side and the other two remain on the tarmac. Then as they came to a bridge over a dry river bed, and came off at the other side, into a village with shops on either side of the road, he noted that the tarmac road ended, and the road was now fully a 'dirt road,' "This is Kezi" called out Tony and Sean recalled how his dad had told many a story of his time at this station. They journeyed on down this road, till rounding a corner, Sean noticed another village come into view, on the right hand side, he noted what appeared to be 'embankments' of earth, and Tony again told him that this was 'Antelope Mine–or what was left of this now deserted mine- that had 'panned out' of gold many years earlier." They drove through, leaving a cloud of dust behind them. As they passed Sun Yet Sen police station, Tony's heart gave a leap, for it held so many memories, both good and bad. He was sad to see the sad state of this once beautiful police camp. "Oh how things Change "Tony said out loud to no-one in particular. No more green hedge...no more green grass... not even white washed stones and the houses were a disgrace...and as he looked he saw what were clearly prostitutes coming and going... "Oh...my precious station" he mused to himself, as they passed on by. Sean could recall many an amusing, and so too sad events his dad had told him about his time here, and was glad that now when recalling these, he could actually picture the places that the events were about, but he too could see that there was no signs of neatness about the place, which he knew must make his dad's heart sad.

They arrived at Nazeby Ranch, and were greeted by many African men, women and children, standing waving and calling out "Ndlovu...Tina bona wena!" (meaning Ndlovu 'we see you') and it was not long before Toby appeared, pushing through the throng, he walked over to Tony, the two looked at each other for a while, and then embraced "Toby" Tony whispered, "How good to see you" to which Toby replied "And I you." Sean could clearly the deep respect that these two had for each other, and watched as his dad went over and shook the hands of all those men women and children, who had turned out to greet them, chatting every now and again to some of those there, and then saw his dad put his hands into his pocket, and come up with sweets, which he handed to each of the children who giggled in glee, thanking him, their eyes all sparkling, and Sean's heart warmed as he saw the respect that his dad had for each and all there assembled, and they for him in return.

Toby, Taz, Sean and Tony walked into the house, and out onto the verandah where they sat and swapped tales, catching up with each other with a mixture of laughter and sadness. Toby took them to where both Bison and Mrs. Jay were buried.

Tony, stood for a while, in quiet contemplation, and then, to nobody in particular, Tony quietly said "Bison, I will see what I can do to repay those who did this to you." Then turning, walked back to the verandah.

Toby and Tazwinga recounted, how since the death of Bison and Mrs. Fay, how their being given the two ranches, how Ngonga's men from the Champion Ranch, frequently carried out 'raids' on the ranches, at first just shooting the odd deer, but recently, had gone to herding, some twenty herd of cattle at a time, off the ranches, onto their own ranch.

"What about the police?" Tony asked, but already knew in his heart what the reply would be. Toby and Tazwinga smiled, and said "Have you forgotten already, Ndlovu...time has made you forget, has it...No....No matter what we report, the police do nothing, these are Ngonga's men - although Inspector Mpofu seems to be seeing what is going on...but what can one man do...especially if he wants to keep his job?"

"Well" Tony said, looking at both of them, "then we'll have to do something about this, won't we?" It was a question that did not need an answer; they all knew what he meant.

They left Toby, and jumping into Tazwinga's Jeep, trundled back to Tazwinga's ranch house, where they unpacked, and as it was now coming up to 5pm, they all retired onto the verandah, and sat watching the sun set, listening to those 'African night' noises, that Tony had missed so much, as they talked about days gone by, and enjoyed a cold glass of Lion Lager together. Tazwinga also told about a rogue elephant, that was causing trouble on the boundary of the Champion and Nazeby ranches. Tony looked up at Sean, and said "Well son, fancy becoming a big game hunter?" Sean's heart leapt, for he relished the thought of being able to return, and tell his brothers, of his exploits, especially if it meant the killing of a rogue elephant, replied "That would be great, with yours and Taz's help of course" but inside he knew that this was to be the ruse, for his dad and Taz to exact revenge on those so called 'war vets'.

After a while, Tony got up and placed a call to his Brother David. After explaining why he was down here, David (who had himself done his regular stint in the Army during those 'war years' in the 'hot bed areas', immediately, stated that he would like to come down and do some Elephant shooting too, which was gratefully accepted by Tony.

37

David was sitting in the lounge of his two bed roomed bungalow, situated a few miles from the Borrowdale Race Course. He sat watching the Sky News, he was grateful for the fact that he had Satellite, to give him broader choice of stations. The phone rang, David slowly got up and ambled over to it, for his years he was fifteen months older than Tony, his hair very grey and starting to thin on top, and a slight bulge was starting on his belly, otherwise his skin was well tanned, as could be seen as he was wearing his usual short sleeved shirt, and shorts and sandals. Picking up the receiver, expecting it to be one of his children, or grandchildren on the other end of the line. As he said "Hello," there came a familiar tone from the other end. "Tony...how are you?" there was a brief pause, then "What....oh I see, yeah if you feel you could use my help, I will run it by Maureen, but sure I could come down...hang on a tick" and he set the receiver down, and ambled into the kitchen where Maureen was busy trying to get a meal together quickly, before the electricity went off. David spoke to her for a few minutes then returned to the phone. Picking up the receiver he said "Sure Tony, no problem - I will leave shortly, drive down- will you be able to meet me at Grey's Inn in Bulawayo?" there was a brief pause, then David said "Sure, will see you soon," and he hung up the phone. He walked to the bedroom and got out an old faded camouflage shirt and trousers, together with some old well worn boots, and putting these into a rucksack, together with some other shorts and shirts and underwear, slung the rucksack over his shoulder, and walked out of the house, to where his old Mercedes was parked, alongside Maureen's VW Beetle, and opening the boot, threw the rucksack in. He closed the boot and returned to the door, where Maureen stood, he kissed her, and she said "Be careful Dear," and David walked back to his car, got in, started the old car up, and slowly moved out of the driveway, and headed out towards Bulawayo.

*****

Tony and Sean, had left Tazwinga, and drove through to Bulawayo, to Grey's Inn, where they had a meal, and sat outside having a beer. They had been sitting there for about two hours, when out from the reception area, strode David. Tony and Sean rose to meet him and after shaking hands, they sat down, David ordered a Coca-Cola, and they caught up with local news, and then they headed off, with David following them in his Mercedes, and headed down to Nazeby.

After the arrival of David, they devised a cunning plan which would be hatched during the next raid. They would be camping nearby, and in order to get Ngonga to physically show up they would use some of their 'illegal weapons' on the raiders.

"Only one way, I see it" Tony explained "If we can catch them stealing the herd, we could use those weapons we are not allowed to have" He winked at Tazwinga, "...to shoot one of the bastards...the news of someone on the ranch using an illegal weapon–will certainly bring old Ngonga down...for he would want to use this, as an excuse to confiscate the ranches, for himself." As he finished, Tazwinga and David were nodding in approval. "Although..." David interjected "What a fine fighting machine we are, you hobbling on your stick Tony, and me with my cataract eye trouble we will have to be careful that we do not kill someone by mistake...thinking they could have been elephants moving in the bush!" they all knew what he meant and all chuckled.

And so the plan was 'hatched' the herdsmen were called together, and a camp was set up, and a 'runner service' to inform the camp when raiders from Champion Ranch came over onto their ranches. All had been told to keep it secret that Tony was here, as he did not want news to filter back to Ngonga.

It was only a matter of days, when late one evening, a report was received, that there had been a 'crossing' and that Ngonga's men were on the ranch. Immediately, Tony, David Tazwinga and Sean, sprang into action. They saddled the four horses, and taking the FN rifles and ammo, they mounted these and set off to intervene.

They rode quietly through the underbrush, and circled in behind the trail, of where Ngonga's men had crossed, and waited for them to return. A few hours passed, when suddenly they heard the mowing of cattle and whistling of Ngonga's herdsmen (his previous freedom fighters) as they pushed the stolen cattle, towards where Tony, David Sean and Tazwinga lay in wait for them.

As they came into view, Tazwinga called out to them, to stop their stealing, and to get off his ranch, his calling out took them by complete surprise, and the one in the lead, immediately went to his AK47 rifle, and shot a burst in Tazwinga's direction. This was all that was needed, for Tony had assigned Sean, whose eyesight was the best and who had the advantage of army training - to take the shot, at whoever fired at them. Tony, David and Tazwinga knew that they would be fired upon.

Sean, had been waiting, the FN in his hand, his eyes peeled waiting for that 'flash' from the gun–he did not have to wait long, as soon as he saw it, he let off a blast - and heard the 'thudding' sound of bullets striking flesh, followed by the howling sound of the target.

There was chaos for a few minutes as the other enemy herdsmen, hurried forward, picked up their fallen comrade, and with much shouting and shooting at nothing...ran off, crossing the Shashani River, back onto Champion Ranch, leaving the cattle where they were. Tony, David, Sean and Tazwinga, herded the cattle together, and waited till dawn's early light, when their assembled 'herdsmen' appeared and drove the cattle back to their pastures. Tony looked over at David, Sean and Tazwinga "Well done son," he said addressing Sean, "right on Target...not a killing blow, but that will give them something to report, and should bring old Ngonga running down" he chuckled "all seems to working like magic" David chuckled, as they mounted and rode off back to the ranch.

The next few days were spent, sending out 'spies' to keep them informed of all developments following the shooting so that the next part of the plan could be initiated. In the mean time all were keeping their eyes peeled for the 'rogue elephant.'

38

Ngonga was sitting at his fine oak desk, in his large impressive office; his young nubile assistant had brought him in his morning coffee, and as usual, had been well squeezed and touched inappropriately by Ngonga. This unsavoury behaviour was part of what those who worked with Ngonga had to put up with. His sexual appetite had never decreased, and he had got through numerous 'assistants' for once he had got his latest catch into his bed, or for that matter onto his couch in his office, he would then tire of that one, and he would raise a false charge to have her dismissed and he would then have the word out for another young newcomer to take her place! Of course it had to be a young girl, for that was what curbed his appetite!

"I do believe that you will have to do some 'overtime' tonight" Ngonga said leeringly at her as he squeezed her round the back. She squirmed, but obediently replied "Of course, Sir." She knew from all reports what the 'overtime' meant, but she wanted to keep her job, for a while longer, as jobs were scarce in Zimbabwe, and the money was well needed, even though she knew that once she had given in to him, it would not be long before she joined the other long list of those who had been 'dismissed.' She broke free, and went back to waiting room, and sat down at her desk. It was not long before the phone rang, she picked it up, and it was the guard at the reception, saying that there was someone from the Champion Ranch, to see Ngonga, and that he was sending him up.

She replaced the phone, and hurried to the door to Ngonga's office and knocked quietly. Ngonga bellowed, "Come in," and as she came into the room, he laughed "Oh, what, you could not wait, eh" and as he rose from his desk, his hands went to the 'flies' of his trousers and started to unzip them "want to do your overtime now - eh?" before he could go any further, she said "Sir...reception is sending up, someone from Champion Ranch, who wants to see you..." before she could say more, Ngonga, halted in mid stride, zipped up his pants once more, and hissed "send him in immediately he gets here" and with a wave of his hand, dismissed the girl. As she turned, walked through the door, back to her desk, closing the door after her, it was only a matter of minutes before the person she was expecting sheepishly came into the room. He saw her and said quietly, "Good Morning, I'm here to see Mr. Ngonga," she rose and escorted him towards the door, she knocked again, and after his shout of 'come in' entered with the man by her side.

As she came in she said "This is the man from Champion Ranch, Sir.." before she could say anything else, he said" GOOD - now go out, close the door - I am not to be disturbed," and beckoning to the man at her side, said "Come, sit" pointing to the chair on the other side of the desk.

The girl made her way out, and the man meekly came and sat down.

"Well, what do you want?" he asked, the man looked up and replied "Sir, there was an incident last week, when we were taking some of Tazwinga and Toby's cattle..." Before he could continue, Ngonga said "INCIDENT...what INCIDENT?" the man looked down at his feet, and continued "we were just about to get the cattle over, when we were told to stop, our leader, opened fire in the direction of the voice ordering us to stop and then..." He paused, until Ngonga bellowed "THEN WHAT?" the man could not look Ngonga in the eyes, and went on to say "Someone, with an automatic rifle, fired back at us, hitting our leader in the right shoulder...we" He could not finish, Ngonga pushed his chair back, and in a stride crossed over and picked the man, up out of his chair, for even with the passing of time Ngonga had still kept himself in reasonable shape, for his age, and especially considering his lifestyle. He raised the man out of the chair, and bellowed "ARE YOU SURE IT WAS AUTOMATIC FIRE?" and when the man nodded, Ngonga released him, and as he fell back into the chair Ngonga screamed "Do not sit back down...hurry back, tell them I will be down in a few days time..." and then musing to himself said "aahh, I will get those other two ranches for myself after all" and he chuckled to himself, then turned, and yelled "WELL...Get out...go tell them to prepare for me...GO!" The man hurried to the door, opened it, and scurried out back to Champion Ranch, as fast as he could. He was only too happy to be away from Ngonga, he had feared that his message may have led to his being 'detained' or worse killed, for such was the fate of many who dared upset Ngonga!

39

The days rolled by since Tony, David, Tazwinga and Sean, had 'ambushed' the rustlers, and they had been waiting for news from their 'spies'. They had heard that the man Sean had shot had been hit in the right shoulder, and that he had gone to the Antelope Hospital to be treated, and that following his release, a man had been sent to make a report to Ngonga.

Tony had said "Wow, what I would give to be a fly on the wall when he makes his report!" "Yeah" replied Tazwinga, just to see the look on Ngonga's face...but I hope he does not bring the army down on us, Ndlovu" and as David and Sean looked over at Tony, Tony continued "No...too proud for that...he will want to come and take these ranches for himself. He will blame either you or Toby for the ambush then make a big deal of it in the press, so he can legally acquire your ranches from you...I know how his mind works."

"So we will just have to patient and wait" he continued "until then, tell you what, Taz, let's take David and Sean and show them the rest of the ranches and the surrounding areas eh" "to which Tazwinga replied, "Sure why not," and arrangement were made for them to 'tour' the area.

*****

Ngonga took the next few days off from work. He stayed at his house, enjoying the favours of the many young girls, he employed, whilst thinking what to do. He finally decided that the best thing for him to do, was to sneak off to Champion Ranch, by himself and together with his comrades from here, go over and take-over the ranches from both Toby and Tazwinga, and then phone the police station at Sun Yet Sen and have them arrested for possession of illegal weapons and make a big issue of the ambush incident, of course leaving out the fact that the ranches taken, will become his!

He took his personal Landrover and drove down to Champion Ranch, feeling quite smug and happy, musing to himself "Pity, Old Bison, and more so that Tony Wood" he spat out that last name with venom "...are not here to see me do this" he smiled happily as he continued his drive, blissfully unaware that his wishes were going to come true!

Tony, David, Sean and Tazwinga, spent the next few days, looking over the ranch, and in particular, following the trail of the rogue elephant that was causing so much trouble along the river, forming the boundary between the Nazeby Ranches and the Champion Ranch. In many places they had to mend the pulled down fences, and on occasions, caught sight of this large, bull elephant. He indeed was a mighty fellow, large tusks, both marked and yellow with age and combat, and due to the drought, his appearance, was of a very light grey indeed, in fact, one would almost say he was white!

Tony looked over at Taz, and whispered "Hey Taz, look it's me, Ndlovu the white elephant" Taz stared through the bushes, and saw for himself this very light grey, giant of a bull elephant, and remembering Tony's African name Ndlovu, nodded back at Tony, whispering "Ahh – Yes - it could well be." Sean, who had been told the story, as a youngster, also recalled it all now that they were here in the presence of this large light grey almost white coloured elephant,

They camped that day at this spot, enjoying watching the huge beast, who although was causing damage, was so remarkable, that neither wanted to end its long life, and rather took pleasure in watching it. But they made sure that they kept' downwind' for should he get a 'whiff' of them, they knew, that they would be in great danger.

It was whilst they were camped here, that they got word that Ngonga had arrived at Champion Ranch, in a RAGE! They knew he would not take long in crossing over to take both Tazwinga's and Toby's ranches for himself.

40

When Ngonga arrived at the Champion Ranch, his comrades, all turned out to wait for him, most in fear of what might happen to them.

But to their surprise, when he did finally get out of his Landrover, although being very short with them, called them into one of the huts, and having sat them down, proceeded to say" Well, since you lot have botched it all up...we now have no option than to call the police in, and have them hear your stories, which I hope will all be the same, that is, that you were in fact scouting to bring back some of OUR cattle that had got over through the fence that this rogue elephant had pulled down, and on trying to get them home, were shot at by...let's say...it was Tazwinga, as he would be the most likely to be believed to have done this, being ex-police himself, he would know how to use an automatic rifle. So let's get your stories straight." Having said that, he went over to the Sear Block, store, and there used the phone to call the Sun Yet Sen police station.

Inspector Mpofu, of the Sun Yet Sen police station, was called to the phone, he took the receiver, and said "Inspector Mpofu- how may I help you?" he paused, then said "Mr. Ngonga, Sir, how are you, ..." and before he could say more, Ngonga cut in "I am at Champion Ranch I want you down here, by yourself, on a very serious matter, I expect you immediately" and with that put down the phone.

Inspector Mpofu, hung up the phone, and wondered just what must have gone wrong now, for Ngonga to come down unannounced. "What could he be planning now!" he mused to himself, then going out of the office said to his staff "I am going to Champion Ranch" and without saying why or for how long, walked out, to the short wheel based Landrover, got into it, and took off in a cloud of dust.

*****

Ngonga had been back at Champion Ranch, for about an hour, when the police Landrover pulled in, stopped and out stepped Inspector Mpofu. He

165

walked up to Ngonga, saluted, and said "Mr. Ngonga, how can I be of help?" Ngonga guided him over to where his comrades were seated, and said "Listen, to what they have to say," and he walked to where a chair had been placed and sat down.

Inspector Mpofu questioned each and every one of Ngonga's comrades, who repeated exactly what Ngonga had told them, and after the last one had had his say, Ngonga said "Now you see, I have had one of my men shot at for no reason, it is lucky that he was not killed...I have tried being neighbourly, but it is obvious that Tazwinga has defied Law and Order, and has had hidden all this time, an automatic weapon, which he is not, BY LAW, (he stressed) allowed to hold, and has used it against one of my men, going about their lawful work." He paused for a moment, to let his words sink in, then continued" That is why I have asked you to come down here, I would like you to accompany me, as we go to Tazwinga's house, where I wish you to arrest him for this breach of Law and Order, and of course, you know by his breaching the law, he has to forfeit his Ranch, which I will duly re-appoint - and if he is working together with that Toby, then he too will suffer the same consequences" he stopped, looking over at Inspector Mpofu, with pride, at what he wanted to have done

"Aahh" Inspector Mpofu mused to himself "that's what this is all about...he wants all three ranches...and now he will get them...and wants me to do his dirty work..." He looked up at Ngonga and said, "Well, Yes Mr. Ngonga, terrible thing to have happened, but of course we are not sure that it was indeed this Tazwinga..." before he could go on, Ngonga, turned on him in a rage "Believe me, Inspector, we have already found out that he is the culprit. I have had 'spies' working for me, at his ranch, and he saw Tazwinga with a FN rifle...No doubt, no one else would have one down here...so you must do you duty" and he left it there, Inspector Mpofu knew to defy this man would mean the end of his career. "Of course, Sir, now that you have told me that, then I now know what you say must be done, so how do you want us to do this?"

Ngonga, looking so pleased with himself, said "well, just today, we came across some spore, suggesting that Tazwinga, and some of his staff, are mending the broken fences that, the rogue elephant, keeps breaking, so he is close at bay, if we split up- you take two of my men, I the other two, and we will circle the area they were last seen at, and catch them–quite possible he will still have his FN rifle with him," he ended with a satisfied grin. "So we must arm ourselves as well "as he handed out AK47 rifles to his men Inspector Mpofu nodded, they split up and went their different ways.

41

Tony, David, Sean and Tazwinga had left their camp and were trailing the elephant on foot. They stopped when he did, and were busy watching the beast, praying that the wind would not change. So intent were they that they were oblivious of what else was going on around them. Sean more so, was so engrossed, in watching this magnificent animal, even though, it was a rogue, he had never seen anything so remarkable, in its natural environment. Now he knew just what a wrench it must have been for his dad and mother to have left this land, to go to England. He too was so engrossed in watching this animal that he was unaware of what else was happening around them.

Tazwinga, Tony, David and Sean, had come upon a bank, and Tazwinga, lay down on the right side of this, where he could clearly see the elephant ahead. Tony had gone further over to the left, with Sean, and David where they could keep an eye on the elephant too. "Well" whispered Tony to Sean, "what you think?" "Wow, Dad" Sean replied, "what a fantastic sight, boy I can see now why you loved it so much out here; with the impala, zebra and wildebeest we have seen, I'm just sorry all the other lads could not have been here to see this remarkable sight..." before he could go on, Tony touched his arm "enjoy son...I'm going to creep back to Tazwinga...keep your eyes open...Ok?" "Sure Dad," Sean replied, and he continued watching the great elephant ahead of him, his Uncle David by his side.

Ngonga and his two comrades soon picked up the trail, that led then straight to the camp, where Tazwinga, Tony, David and Sean had been. One of Tazwinga's herdsmen had been left in charge of the camp, Ngonga and his two comrades, quickly, bound him up, and after a beating, ascertained that Tazwinga had gone, and were shown the direction, in search of the elephant. He never mentioned who was with Tazwinga, and Ngonga presumed, that if anyone was with him it would be just another 'servant,' so turning to his two comrades he said "stay here with him… do not let him loose till I return" and with that, he marched off up the trail, with his own automatic rifle at the ready.

Ngonga, with all his police training, and then his training as a terrorist leader, could follow a trail quite well, and do so, without causing too much noise, his heart was beating faster, as he was already thinking how he could use his two newly to be gained ranches for his sordid lifestyle.

He slowly moved through the bush, and as he came round a corner froze, for there in front of him, he suddenly saw a figure…lying down in the grass…he watched for a while till he could be certain, that it was Tazwinga…" what is he doing lying down there?" he mused to himself, and then suddenly his attention went to movement to the side, and there…another figure, more rotund, and heavy set, an EUROPEAN…"who the hell could this be" he said to himself, then "Oh, so he has got some white man's help, has he, too bad, will take them both…"

And with that, he jumped out from where he was, cocking his AK 47 rifle and making sure the safety catch was off and shouted out "Stay where you are, do not move, I am armed and will shoot you.

Both Tony and Tazwinga froze, as they both recognized this voice, and knew just how certain he would be to shoot them. They lay perfectly still, and heard footsteps behind them. The voice they knew so well continued "OK, you two, I know you Tazwinga (he spat), but who is the white man (he used the term as if it was a dirty word) with you? Go on, both very slowly roll over…" and his voice suddenly ended as he saw Tony roll over…" NDLOVU" he screamed "YOU…" He paused to catch his breath…this was better than he could have ever dreamed of, here was his chance to get both of these men he hated so, he gathered himself, "Hah, this is truly a wonderful day…that I have delivered to me …both of you" he laughed out loud, both Tony and Tazwinga, held up their hands, to silence him, knowing that the bull elephant was so close at hand, but Ngonga fearing that they were about to 'jump him' let go a burst of fire over their heads. Then two things happened at once, the first was that the wind changed, the second was that the bull elephant caught their scent, and with an almighty trumpeting, charged towards them.

42

Inspector Mpofu, had been circling with the two comrades of Ngonga's when they suddenly saw the large bull elephant, ahead of them. At the sight of this, the one comrade, decided that enough was enough and he quietly retreated, and backed off towards Champion Ranch. The other remained, but was in no mood to go any further, so hung back behind Inspector Mpofu, who in himself was not too keen to get to close to this rogue elephant.

As the two of them stood there, they suddenly heard the voice of Ngonga ring out "stay where you are, do not move, I am armed and will shoot you." Who could he be talking to? They stared through the bush trying to make him out, but beyond the elephant, there was also a large bank, and they could see nothing. They kept very still. Then they heard the bust of automatic rifle fire, and in an instant, the bull elephant, turned and trumpeting, charged towards the bank. The scene was so terrifying that the remaining comrade, bolted like a scalded dog, off into the bush, running to join his comrade back at Champion Ranch. Inspector Mpofu stood still, he could do little else, he was unarmed. He waited to see what would happen.

*****

Sean and David had been peacefully, watching the big bull elephant ahead of them, when Tony had left them, Sean wishing that his brothers, Barry, Garth, Kirk, Wayne and Grant, could have been here to take in this wonderful sight, when he suddenly heard a voice say "Stay where you are, do not move, I am armed and will shoot you." He moved slowly, turning to look over to where his dad and Tazwinga lay, and then noticed another African come out from the bush, holding an automatic rifle, which he had heard cocked, and although he could not hear what else was being said, saw both his dad and Tazwinga, turn slowly over to face this man, and noticed now when his dad turned, the man stopped in his tracks. He noticed that both his dad and Tazwinga had held up their hands–towards this third person, as if suggesting that he back down or be quiet, then saw and heard, the burst of gunfire, and saw the bullets go over the heads of his dad and Tazwinga, and before he could do anything else, he heard the loud trumpeting of the rogue elephant, at the same time he felt a breeze on his face, and knew that the wind had changed, then heard the thunder as this giant bull elephant charged towards where his Dad and Tazwinga lay, held by this stranger. He could not do anything for fear this stranger may shoot, so just lay there his head spinning, all his army career training, including his time in both Afghanistan, and Iraq, going through his mind, waiting to take his shot, at this stranger, but David, having been in many similar situations in his Army Call ups in the Mana Pools area, put his hand onto Sean's and whispered "Wait...bide your time, make sure you can get a good killing shot, I'm watching Tony and Taz, soon as I see a sign I will tap you...You take your shot," but before Sean could even do so, the events were turned.

Ngonga, smirked, as he walked towards where Tazwinga and Tony lay, "Ha, NDLOVU, how I have waited for this moment...you no doubt thought that I would serve my sentence in prison for what I did...oh no, my big white elephant...you were wrong, I got this job instead..." he chuckled out loudly, and then stopped, and turned, as the great big rogue bull elephant, crashed round the embankment

And headed for him "NO" he screamed, "NO...NDLOVU...NOT AGAIN..." But before he could say anymore, the great beast had whacked him with its trunk, knocking him to the ground, whereupon it too stopped, turned, and knelt down on the figure in front of him, doing so his large yellow stained tusk, speared through Ngonga's stomach.

Tony, grabbed at his FN rifle, and taking careful aim, fired a burst into this great beast in front of him, he managed to pierce the brain, and get bullets into the heart of this beast, and with a bellow it fell to its side, the tusk that had speared Ngonga, now raised up with Ngonga hanging on it. He dangled on the end of the tusk, hanging there in his death throes.

Sean and David had by this time run to Tony's side, and as both the rogue elephant, and Ngonga died, Tazwinga touched Tony's arm, "So it was, Ndlovu ...he died, just as he had dreamt," and Tony understood just what he meant.

It was at this time that Inspector Mpofu, appeared, and took in the awful scene in front of him. Tazwinga, of course introduced Tony, his Brother

David and his son Sean, as being visitors from England on Holiday, and of course Inspector Mpofu, was unaware, of Tony's background, nor what had transpired in the past. He heard from Tazwinga, about the raids, and finally said "Well, it's a terrible accident...no blame...rogue elephants do this...but of course I will have to confiscate those FN rifles...but with no charges, I assure you. What I will be doing is arresting those on Champion Ranch, and with Mr. Ngonga now deceased, what I will do, is hand over the Champion Ranch, to the locals in the area...I am sure they will cause you no trouble. "With that and handshakes, Inspector Mpofu retired.

Two days later, news filtered through that Champion Ranch had, indeed been handed over to the locals of Sear Block Area, and it was announced in the Bulawayo Newspaper and Local Radio, that Ngonga had met a terrible death, by a rogue elephant, whilst visiting the Champion Ranch.

Tony, David and Sean, stayed for a few more days with Tazwinga, then, journeyed once more with him, up to see Toby at Nazeby, and to say a final farewell to both Bison and Mrs. Jay, before going onto Bulawayo Airport to catch their plane back to England. The farewells to Tazwinga were sad indeed, as they were with Toby, for all knew, that all in their sixties probably would never be another re-union. But happy they were, as was Cheryl, on hearing that neither Tony, David, Taz nor Sean had to resort to killing anyone, and that the end of Ngonga at least, would mean a temporary reprieve for both Tazwinga and Toby. Parting too, with his brother David was sad, but Tony was thankful for their brief escapade, and thanked him, wishing him a safe journey back to Harare and best wishes to Maureen his wife and to his children and grandchildren. They entered the airport, with Taz and David going up to the balcony, to say their final goodbyes, waving till Tony and Sean had boarded the plane, then watched as the plane taxied down the runway and took off.

Epilogue

Tony sat watching the news, and could not believe what he had heard, he called to Cheryl - "Guess what, sweetheart?" and without waiting for a reply, continued "They have had an African Conference, would you believe it, all the other African Governments, have called upon Zimbabwe - to restore Law and Order immediately and return farms seized unlawfully. They do think that there could be more distribution of land, but that it must be done lawfully and if Bugabe does not, they will kick him out of summit, and Commonwealth!"

"Would you believe it - let's hope that after all this time, commonsense will prevail" and he tailed off, in his private thoughts,....thoughts of his beloved Africa, and how that at last, although he knew that just because they have said so, did not mean that Bugabe would do it, but he might consider the implications, realizing, the dire state of his economy, and pressure from all surrounding African states, that he would be on his own- and maybe....just maybe. .there might be light at the end of the tunnel, and he hoped so, for the sake of his brother, and nephews and nieces who were still living there. "Shame, Bison and Mrs. Jay, could not have lived to see this" he mused to himself, as he walked over to the window, and looked up at the night sky, and then his thoughts returned once again, to the peaceful, fun days, that Africa had all been about.

"Aaagh, Ndlovu, "he mused to himself" maybe at last you will now find some peace and those dreadful nightmares will end, and maybe... just maybe, there will be peace again in Africa... peace for the peoples and animals... yes even for rhinos and elephants," he laughed quietly to himself and continued, "Yeah, even for Ndlovu an old...White Elephant!"

ABOUT THE AUTHOR

Peter Good was born in Kenya. He was educated in Kenya and later Dar-es-Salaam, Tanzania. His childhood years were spent with his parents, brothers and sister in the isolated mining and farming areas of Kenya, and it was here that his fondness for the 'bush' life, and wild animals grew.

In 1959 his parents moved to Southern Rhodesia (now known as Zimbabwe) where he joined the British South Africa Police Force. He spent his entire service in the Matabeleland Province. He served as Public Prosecutor in the local Magistrate Courts for five years.

It was whilst at the District stations, in the Matabeleland Province that he proceeded to learn the customs and language of the local populace, even joining them in their 'beer drinks' - something that won their respect, which paid off during the troubled times of 'terrorist' activity.

He came to England in 1977, where he has remained since, but still regards Africa as his 'home'.

This is his first story, drawn from an idea based loosely on actual events witnessed during his police career, and other incidents, both experienced and heard, during his life in a 'Changing Africa'.

Lightning Source UK Ltd.
Milton Keynes UK
UKOW051159120712

195869UK00001B/17/P